I0557359

THE BONE DOLL

Book I | The Ruthenian Chronicle

Rebecca Ganesh

Copyright © 2025 Rebecca Ganesh

All rights reserved

The characters and events portrayed in this book are fictitious. Any similarity to real persons, living or dead, is coincidental and not intended by the author.

No part of this book may be reproduced, or stored in a retrieval system, or transmitted in any form or by any means, electronic, mechanical, photocopying, recording, or otherwise, without express written permission of the publisher.

ISBN-13: 979-8-9997679-0-5 (ebook), 979-8-9997679-1-2 (paperback)

Cover design by: RCG CoverDesign
Library of Congress Control Number: 2025916950
Printed in the United States of America

CONTENTS

CHAPTER 1
Constellations

Syra traced the constellations in the sky. The Glacier, the Sled, the Earth Deer... A crease formed between her brows as she followed the stars which formed a straight line to the Unmoving Man, who sat at the sky's apex and winked strangely. Her gaze trailed along that line of stars again – a perfect line and a blinking star. A star that was usually steady.

A chilly evening wind played with loose strands of her hair, and she pressed her lips into a line. She knew that perfect line meant something, but no matter how much she opened herself up to her magic, she found no meaning.

"A line," she whispered. "What is a line with a blinking end?"

Perhaps a more creative woman would have been able to interpret the omen on its own. But Syra wanted her magic to work, just like her grandfather had told her it would. Her scowl deepening, she concentrated harder, willing visions to appear.

Nothing.

Her magic was weak, and even a simple search for omens eluded her.

Syra sighed. She might be a *vidutana* – a sky shaman amongst her people, the Sarnoks – but the sky spirits had not blessed her with skill or power. And though her grandfather had tried to teach her, there was only so much a sculptor could do with dull tools. When her grandfather had passed last year, none of the other *vidutana* thought Syra's powers warranted honing.

So, she came out here at least twice a week in hopes that she could learn on her own, if she continued to practice what her grandfather had taught her – how to read omens, how to seek visions and prophesies, and how to draw magical power. Alas, it had been more than a year, and Syra noticed no improvements. Some nights, she spent worrying that her grandfather should have offered his time to a more worthy *vidutana*. Other nights, she put those thoughts from her head and kept trying, hoping that she would grow more powerful eventually.

Rising to her feet, she dusted the mud and dead grass off her clothes and headed southward across the tundra, which was patchy with snow and spring lichen. Her clan's camp lay a mile away beneath the arrow of the Sirtian Hunter constellation, enveloped by trees through which her clan's reindeer herds foraged and dogs scavenged,. She held the image in her mind's eye as she walked.

She crossed a still-frozen brook, silver and cracked with spring's incoming warmth. And then her gloved hand closed around the hilt of her belt knife as she caught sight of someone moving in the dark.

This stranger didn't care about stealth or subterfuge, striding towards her with his head held high. As he neared, the starlight illuminated his features. Her gaze glued to him – and not because he was an unfamiliar man approaching at night. And not because he was a Ruthenian. She had seen pale-skinned Ruthenians before, even if they preferred to stick to their trading posts at the western edges of the tundra. She stared because she had never seen anyone with hair like orangebush lichen, which he left uncovered despite the cold. He was like a fire spirit walking the earth, just without the flame.

"Do you glare at everyone you meet?" he said in accented but clear Sarnok.

Syra stiffened. "Only men who wander in the dark."

"I didn't mean to be out here this late," he replied. "But I got turned around and haven't been able to find what I was looking for."

She stepped backwards. This one spoke in riddles and half-truths, just like a trickster spirit. Maybe he was a ghost. But even if he was just a man, he certainly wasn't one a lone woman wanted to deal with in the middle of the night.

"Can you help me?" the Ruthenian continued. "I'm looking for the Lame Wolf clan."

She fidgeted with her knife's handle. What could this orange-haired Ruthenian want with her clan? Certainly, it was nothing good. Gingerly, she shifted to the right, trying to make her way around him. "No clan wants a Ruthenian visitor in the middle of the night."

"I–" He looked like he was actually considering that. "I can wait until morning to enter their camp. But I don't know *where* they are. You're the first person I've seen in two days, and I was hoping you could point me in their direction so I'm not wandering around aimlessly for another two days."

"I don't know where they are," she lied, finally stepping clear of him and striding purposefully away.

The Ruthenian jogged after her. "If you don't know– If you wouldn't mind– I could use some company and somewhere to rest."

Company? She shot him a dirty look over her shoulder. *Company?* What did Ruthenian women do when they met strange men in the middle of the night? If they shared their *company*, Syra would eat her own foot. Pivoting on her heel, she drew her belt knife. "Get back," she warned. "You're lucky I haven't gutted you."

"Wait, wait." He held up both hands, faltering. "You're just the only person out here, and I thought you might share a campfire and conversation."

Her face heated. The more he said, the worse it sounded. Her fingers tightened on her knife. "Come any closer – or follow me – and you'll have this knife in your throat."

He licked his lips, rubbing his palms on the front of his coat – black patterned with interlocking blue circles. His knife gleamed at his side, its handle freshly wrapped in new leather. Either it was new or he never used it. He wasn't a warrior, a fact that might just save her skin. He still held up his hands. "All right," he acquiesced. "I won't follow. And I'll stay right here. But can you just tell me which direction–"

Syra wasn't waiting around. She darted around him and then ran, leaving the Ruthenian man flustered and gaping like a dead fish.

CHAPTER 2
The Bone Doll

Tying her hood tighter around her face, Syra walked out onto the river with her brother Ngarka and sister Raya. Though they were no longer in the dead of winter when the sun did not rise, the river was still frozen; and it would remain that way until summer. Partially obscured by drifting snow, a bone bobber peaked out of the ice.

Syra tilted her head and paused. "I hope there are more fish than last time."

"The more you worry," said Raya, "the more unlucky you are."

"I don't think that's true," Syra said.

Raya gave her a wan smile. Like everyone in the Lame Wolf clan, she was thinner than she had been before winter, her cheek bones angling sharply out. "It might be. You never know."

Syra snorted, shaking her head. "The fish won't catch themselves. And *nyebya* needs the food."

They didn't discuss their mother's lingering cough, or how she had lost more weight than anyone else this winter. They had spoken about it enough this past season. So instead, they turned to their fishing. Stepping onto the frozen river, Syra and her siblings broke the ice with their harpoons. Raya picked up shards of ice and flicked them and her older brother and sister. Syra knocked her with the blunt end of her harpoon, while Ngarka ignored them both and pulled the bobber from the narrow hole they'd made. Carefully but quickly, he extracted the net. A half-dozen muksun and a yellow-speckled pike flapped around, trapped.

"See?" Ngarka offered a gap-toothed smile. "More than last

time."

Syra cocked an eyebrow at her sister. "My worrying isn't unlucky."

"You got lucky this one time," Raya protested.

Stripping their gloves, the siblings delicately peeled the fish from the net and then dropped them in a canvas bag. All the while, Raya muttered insults about how slow her siblings were at freeing the fish.

Her bare hands burning from the cold, Syra plucked the final muksun from the net just as her sister whistled low under her breath. "Munku is coming."

"Someone is in trouble," Ngarka said.

The Lame Wolf Pathfinder, the clan's leader, sat in her sled, drawn by a pair of reindeer with bells on their harnesses. Munku tapped her reindeers sides and rumps to steer her sled to the very edge of the river, where she stopped and stood. Munku was a giantess of a woman, who crowned herself with the preserved head of a gray wolf, its hide cascading down her back. All who beheld her paused.

"Syra, come with me," she demanded.

Syra just stood there. The Pathfinder had better, stronger *vidutana* than her to serve as advisors. Syra couldn't think of any good reason that Munku wanted her.

Ngarka elbowed her, muttering from the corner of his mouth, "Go."

Swallowing, Syra dropped the fish into the bag and then staggered across the river. She opened her mouth to speak, but Munku cut her off.

"I need you at camp." The Pathfinder gestured to the sled. "Now."

You asked questions of Munku sparingly, and you argued only in desperate situations. So, Syra sat in the back of the Pathfinder's sled, pulling her knees to her chest. Munku tapped her reindeers on the rump.

They rode across melting snow and slick mud back to the campsite. About 60 Lame Wolf clan members lived in ten *myas*, conical tents made of reindeer fur and wood. They were transportable and easy to set up, perfect residences for following the reindeer herds as they migrated south in the winter and north in the summer. Now, the camp was alive with men and women chipping ice off their belongings, or chopping firewood. A cloud-white dog chased alongside Munku's sled for a moment, barking at the reindeer, but it eventually ran off.

Munku's *mya* was the tallest and widest, marked with wolfskulls that dangled above the doorflap. She had killed at least two of them this winter when the starving beasts tried to eat the clan's reindeer. Munku had then skinned, boiled, and eaten them. Yet another reason why any Sarnok – Lame Wolf clan or not – thought twice before crossing the woman.

"Inside." Munku left the sled and crawled into her *mya*.

Following her into the tent, Syra was greeted by the smell of heavy smoke and boiling fish so strong that her eyes watered. Next, she noticed a man with hair like orangebush lichen, sitting on the wolfskin rug. She bit back a curse. That Ruthenian. He *had* found them. And went straight to their Pathfinder? She sucked on her teeth. If he had gotten her in trouble with Munku, she would personally blacken both his eyes.

Loosening the top button on her coat, Munku sat on a low, cushioned stool before her hearth. "Sit, Syra. This will take awhile."

Syra knelt. That man approached her in the middle of the night and asked to share her company. Like a pervert. She should have gutted him. Because now, who knew what he had told Munku? That she had been rude to him – a guest? Well, he deserved it.

"This is Viktor Igorevich." Munku gestured to the orange-haired Ruthenian, who sat with his legs folded in front of him and wore an entirely innocent expression. "He comes on behalf of a Ruthenian lord, seeking our aid."

I can't help him. Syra kept her mouth shut and refused to look at the Ruthenian. *Viktor.*

"A forest spirit has broken free of its domain and now

threatens to destroy human homes," Munku summarized. "Viktor seeks a means to subdue this spirit and return it to its woods."

A cold, hard lump settled in Syra's stomach.

The Pathfinder held up her hand before Syra had a chance to speak. "I'm not asking you to give it up. I'm asking you to help him."

Viktor watched the two of them, his expression almost oblivious. Syra knew he could understand Sarnok. But did he know what they were talking about?

"I buried the thing," said Syra.

Munku sighed and then spoke slowly as though to a petulant child. "Then, dig it up and help him. That is not so hard. He knows we have it, and he has offered to pay us."

Syra's throat constricted. The clan could use the money after the winter they had endured. But she couldn't fathom using *it*. "I dig up that thing and risk everyone within a hundred feet of me. You remember last winter before I buried it. How it gave us nightmares and lured Yeyka out into the wilderness and sent half of our herd running to their deaths."

"Exactly," Munku said. "We have half the herd we used to. Viktor has offered us 1,000 silver coins in exchange for the Bone Doll. With that money, we can purchase reindeer from the other clans and rebuild."

Syra turned to Viktor for the first time. "It whispers and drives you mad. You can't carry it."

"*You* can," the Pathfinder said. "It has never affected you. Your grandfather thought it was because you shared his magic."

That lump of ice in Syra's stomach grew even larger, and she pressed her hand against her abdomen. Syra's grandfather had been one of the most powerful shamans in Sarnok history, capable of unfathomable feats. Before Syra had been born, before her father had been born, her grandfather had traversed the sky to where the stars lived. There, he had found the bones of a sky spirit and, from it, he fashioned a little doll. The doll looked like nothing more than a carved sculpture of a genderless Sarnok in their reindeer-skin clothes, but this little doll held untold magic.

Her grandfather could do almost anything by using its power.

Now, it was scourge, a curse.

Except to Syra.

"You will carry the Bone Doll for him," Munku said. "The Ruthenians will never touch it."

Syra felt exposed. Munku was supposed to be her ally, but she was willing to feed Syra to a wolf with orange fur for enough silver.

"The Bone Doll will remain safely in your possession," agreed Viktor. "I have no desire to take it from you. I'm only here to facilitate a mutually beneficial exchange between the Lame Wolf clan and the Lord of Zoldrovya."

Syra clenched her fists until they ached. "What about me? I do not want to go."

"You are the only one who can," the Pathfinder said.

"I do not care about the Ruthenians and their woodland spirit."

"I can offer an advance," Viktor said. "250 *grivna*. In good faith."

"Your offer is generous, Viktor Igorevich," Munku said before turning back to Syra. "Your clan needs this. If you will not do it for us, then do it for yourself. Your grandfather used the Bone Doll to augment his powers. Perhaps learning to use it will make you stronger."

Syra took a deep breath, doubting the Pathfinder's logic.

"I've decided," Munku declared, setting her jaw in a way that brooked no argument. "You're taking the Bone Doll to this Lord of Zoldrovya. Bind the spirit back to the forest, and bring back the silver we need to rebuild our herd." She turned to Viktor. "We will gladly accept your advance."

Syra opened her mouth to object but no sound emerged. All she could do was stiffly crawl out of Munku's *mya* before she found her voice and said something she would regret.

CHAPTER 3
A Long Three Weeks

If Viktor thought Ruthenia was cold in early springtime, it was nothing compared to the eastern tundra. Here, the cold threatened to gnaw off your skin and freeze your bones. Repressing a shiver, he set his pack on the ground. He pulled out sacks of preserved food, opening them to show to the Sarnoks. Dried apple slices, cranberries, a round of hard cheese, and walnuts. It wasn't much – only as much as he could carry – but after a cold winter, the Lame Wolf clan eagerly accepted the gift. Viktor needed one of their religious artifacts, their Bone Doll, and so he wanted to garner good will.

Alas, the person he needed the most good will from was unimpressed.

"You know, I'm actually quite a pleasant travel companion," he assured the Sarnok woman, Syra, who was packing her bag. Viktor didn't actually know that. He usually traveled alone. But he couldn't imagine he was nearly as aggravating as she was making him out to be. "I am well-versed in a multitude of conversation topics. And as you can tell, I speak Sarnok proficiently."

She didn't even look at him as she secured her bedroll to the bottom of her pack.

Viktor repressed a sigh. She clearly didn't want to accompany him. It was evident in the way she silently but aggressively slung her pack over her shoulders.

He donned his pack, which was considerably lighter now that he had given away most of the food he had brought, and started out of the Lame Wolf clan's camp.

Snow patches melted and then refroze beneath the harsh

tundra sun; and a fine fuzz of brown grass tried to claw its way out of the snow and ice. A murder of crows cawed as they flew overhead, forming a broken V in the pale gray sky. The Sarnok woman followed after him, trudging with the speed of a reanimated corpse. She just didn't look at him, nor did she speak. They traveled like that for hours while Viktor told himself it didn't matter how quiet she was, so long as she carried the Bone Doll for him.

For his father.

Viktor wasn't surprised that his father's demand for magic to control a *leshy* came with a catch. When he had learned of the magical doll, Viktor had hoped that he could simply purchase the talisman and not risk anyone's safety. But of course, all Igor Sviatopolkovich's schemes ended up involving human collateral. This time, it was Syra who had to carry the doll. Viktor just wished he wasn't always there to witness the damage his father's plans wrought.

I'm just doing what I'm told. The lie didn't make him feel better.

Finally, Viktor stopped, waiting for his Sarnok companion to catch up. When she did, she gazed straight through him like he was a ghost. He bit the inside of his cheek. She couldn't ignore him for the next three weeks. Taking one look at her expression, however, he realized that she would try.

Best to get past this sooner rather than later.

"May I see the Bone Doll?" he asked.

"No."

"I just want to know if you have it," he said. "So I know we aren't walking 150 miles for no reason."

She surveyed the tundra, her lips pressed into a thin line. "I wouldn't be walking with you at all if I didn't have it."

True, he admitted, though her words stung. Really, he couldn't be that odious. He pressed on. "Have you used it before?"

Her lips twitched and her eyes narrowed, focused on the horizon. Then, she said, "Aren't we going somewhere?"

"Zoldrovya."

"We won't get there if we just stand here," she said flatly.

He nodded in defeat. This was going to be a long three weeks.

Again, she fell into step several yards behind him. As the sun passed its zenith and into the west, they passed a rocky expanse filled with reindeer bones. His hair stood on end, and he tried not to think about what had caused such devastation.

Syra broke her silence in order to enlighten him. "This is what the Bone Doll does. It drives you mad. It drove these reindeer into a stampede, and they crushed each other."

He grimaced and started walking faster.

Beyond the reindeer graveyard, the ground turned into mud that splashed them no matter how gently they stepped. A series of wolf tracks crossed through. Viktor hoped they weren't too fresh, but he didn't ask Syra for her input. He doubted she would give it.

Soon enough, a dirt road appeared. Though deeply rutted and overgrown, it led back to the lands held by the Princess of Rodgorod. He knew he would be a better companion once they entered Ruthenia. He would know better where to go and how to travel comfortable. His Sarnok companion still said nothing. They took the Ruthenian road westward until sunset when they made camp in a shallow ditch lined with barren pine trees.

Viktor and Syra worked in parallel to set up camp. He unpacked the last of his food, while Syra lit a fire. He sat by her fire and pulled out his provisions. Syra unwrapped a salted fish and cut it in half, ignoring his offer to share food.

"Don't put your bedroll too close," she said.

Viktor raised an eyebrow. "Worried about my snoring?"

She propped her elbows on her knees, chewing an apple slice.

Taking a swig from his waterskin, Viktor tried to regroup. Of course, he had had no plans of sleeping *too* close to Syra. But certainly he wasn't so reprehensible as to be exiled to the other side of the camp. His jaw tightened. Except Syra *had* just exiled him. He lowered his head, his throat aching. *I truly am the last person she wants to be near.*

"I meant what I said in your Pathfinder's tent," he said. "I don't want your Bone Doll. I'm just here to make sure that it reaches Zoldrovya."

Syra said nothing

Viktor sighed as though she had leveled an accusation. He didn't *have* to participate in his father's machinations. He traveled to get away from his father. But it never worked like that. Viktor had no money unless his father gave it to him. So, if Viktor wanted the funds to travel, he needed his father. And so he needed to participat in Igor Sviatopolkovich's games.

"If I had a choice, I would leave your relic in the tundra," he said. "But we all have false choices. Live on the street like a vagabond or do someone else's bidding."

"Help a useless Ruthenian," she said, "or let your clan suffer more."

Viktor grimaced. "Surely, I am not *useless*."

"I've never met a Ruthenian who wasn't."

"How many Ruthenians have you met?" he asked.

"Enough." She shrugged. "We trade with them in the summer. They are too scared to leave their camps."

Viktor patted his chest. "Well, *I* am brave. I came all the way out to your clan's camp."

Syra snorted. "Brave? I've seen mice braver than you."

"It must have been a very brave mouse," he said. "Heroic, almost."

Her lips quirked, and Viktor thought she might be smiling. But she sobered quickly. Then, she unbuttoned her distinctive coat – made of reindeer hide and trimmed in an intricately woven wool. Viktor had never seen – nor thought about – what lay beneath a Sarnoks' coat. Her trousers were, in fact, coveralls that extended over her chest and tied behind her neck. They hung loosely off her, made for a woman who hadn't faced a lean winter.

From the front pocket of her coveralls, she withdrew something small and ivory-colored.

"You wanted to see it," she said.

It was the Bone Doll. As tall as his palm was wide, the Bone

Doll was carved from bone, in the shape of a Sarnok in their coat and overalls, a small knife in their hand. The fire spluttered as the figurine took on a faint glow of its own. Gooseflesh puckered across Viktor's skin.

Viktor arched an eyebrow. Was this what he earned for making her almost-smile?

"My grandfather made it," Syra said. "He used its magic for all sorts of things, including protecting our clan from angry spirits. But now, it's angry."

Viktor looked at the doll and then at Syra, her face painted in hues of blue and red. Magic and fire. "How does it protect you?"

Her fingers tightened on the figurine. "If winds would not stop, my grandfather would bind the angry spirit back to the air. If a spirit flooded our campsite, he could bind the offending spirit back to its rain cloud."

That was exactly what he had heard from the Parmians who had told him that the Lame Wolves had a powerful artifact that could control errant spirits. And that was exactly what his father wanted. But his father wanted more.

"It doesn't do any of that anymore," she finished.

Why? The word was hot on his tongue, but Viktor knew from the flint in her eyes that she would answer no more questions. And so, he nodded as though he understood.

Syra stuffed the Bone Doll back into her pocket. She pulled out her bedroll and flattened it on the other side of the fire. She lay with her back to him, again pretending as though he did not exist at all.

This would be a long three weeks, he thought for the hundredth time.

CHAPTER 4

Reindeer Moss

Syra endured three days of endless walking across muddy tundra, overflowing streams, and sharp gravel. By the fourth day, the rough road carried them into a pine and spruce forest where snow still clung to the trees' roots. The place smelled of rot.

She walked a dozen or more paces behind Viktor, but she *still* heard him humming. She had half a mind to close the distance between them and choke him. Then he'd be quiet. Syra had been all but forced to help him. Wasn't that bad enough? What had she done to deserve listening to his incessant noise-making?

Syra hung back further to snack on some berries she had spotted growing in the underbrush. As she crouched there, she remembered how skinny Raya looked. Her stomach twisted. Maybe listening to Viktor's humming was better than dealing with her homesickness. She started walking again. Her belly hurt whenever she thought about her family, their *mya*, her clan, the reindeer...

So wrapped up in her thoughts of home, Syra bumped into the orange-haired Ruthenian, who had stopped along the path. Grunting her displeasure, she sidestepped him and folded her arms across her chest.

Viktor jerked his chin towards a deeply-gouged tree trunk. "Might be a bear."

Any Sarnok worth their marrow could identify animal markings; and a bear wouldn't cut that deep into a tree, not to sharpen its claws anyway. But before she could identify the marks, Viktor was talking again.

"It doesn't look too fresh," he said – clearly to himself because she wasn't responding. "Hopefully, it's not too close."

She set her jaw and glared ahead. Whatever it was, Viktor would be the one eaten. He clearly wasn't the brightest. Viktor began walking again, his hand on the hilt of his belt knife. Then, she followed him.

Alas, no animals appeared that day, sparing Viktor the fate of becoming some creature's dinner.

By sunset, a fierce northern wind swept through the trees. Gritting her teeth, Syra wished she was back in her *mya*, sheltered by reindeer hides and warmed by a fire. And the place Viktor found for a campsite was lackluster. Only a few thorny, leafless bushes served as cover, letting the wind buffet them mercilessly. Viktor cut branches and then struck his unmarred blade against his flint. But the fire was stubborn, the wind blowing it out repeatedly. Syra kept her advice to herself, setting out her bedroll. The Ruthenian finally got it.

"All I have is a small bag of dried bilberries," Viktor said.

Syra would have complained, except he had given the rest of his food to her clan. It seemed wrong to belittle him for that kindness.

So, she begrudgingly accepted half of the berries, and shared the last of her salted fish. It wasn't enough, but she knew better than to complain in lean times.

After their meager supper, she crawled into her sleeping roll with her back facing him, as she had every night since this ludicrous journey had started. She listened to him set out his own bedding – across the fire from her – and tried to read the stars through the trees. Her exhaustion caught up to her eventually and she drifted to sleep.

Her sleep wasn't easy. Syra tossed and turned, plagued by nightmares that she couldn't remember. After one particularly frightening episode, she sat up in her bedroll, panting. The fire was nothing but embers now, and the air was frigid. Her teeth chattering, Syra rubbed her arms in an attempt to get warm.

That was when she noticed humming against her abdomen.

She unbuttoned her coat. It was the Bone Doll. Syra slid it free from her pocket, and its carvings glowed beneath her fingers. She had never heard it *hum* before.

Something moved in the forest. Carefully extricating herself from her bedroll, she padded towards the movement.

There, amongst the trees and shrubs, a creature crouched. It had hair like gleaming copper and a heavy brow that shadowed its rowan berry-colored eyes. Slowly, it peeled back its bloated, red lips to reveal a set of teeth filed down to points. It made a clicking sound like a cicada and shuffled towards her on its feet and knuckles.

Syra staggered back. This was a spirit, but not one she knew. And she did not want to risk an encounter with an unknown creature. Her fingers tightened on the Bone Doll. She remembered how her grandfather, his clothes rattling with wolves' teeth, bound a snow spirit to its storm, ending a seven-day blizzard. Syra was not strong enough for that magic, so she tried something else – her grandfather's dispelling chant.

The world is ash, our hearts are stone.
Go! Return to your rightful home.

She hissed as the Bone Doll suddenly seared her hand, the pain racing up her forearm. What was happening? She concentrated and said the words again.

The red creature clicked. Then, the trees rustled and it was gone.

The pain in her hand eased, and the Bone Doll stopped glowing. She stared at it for a long moment. Had her magic ... worked? Maybe Munku was right: the Bone Doll *would* augment her powers?

Viktor propped himself up on his elbow. "What is it?"

"Nothing," she lied. "I just had to pee."

Syra turned away from him and pulled the blanket over herself. The Bone Doll had hummed. And then that creature appeared. A shiver passed through her. Had it warned her?

She closed her eyes and tried to think of something else.

She didn't manage to sleep the rest of the night, so she

dragged even further behind Viktor the next day. And she had to stop every once in a while to scrub the exhaustion from her eyes. When she did, she glanced around, searching for any other strange spirits but finding none.

When she looked back to the road, Viktor was walking slowly, his gait slightly stilted like had a hidden limp. She had nearly caught up with him despite her own trudging pace. Syra tried to slow even further, but then Viktor stopped. Sighing loudly, she let him fall in alongside her.

"Do the Sarnok tell any stories?" Viktor asked.

Syra gave him a sideways glare. "What are you talking about?"

"Do you tell stories – about the gods or heroes – to pass the time?" he said.

"All people do that."

"Tell me one."

She shifted her pack on her shoulders. The man with the orangebush hair wanted to hear a story? Fine. "I'll tell you a children's story. Hopefully, you'll be able to grasp it."

"I do hope so." The corner of his lips twitched.

"Dog lived by himself in the southern forest," she began. "And he was lonely. So he left his house and went to look for a friend. He first met Eagle, who lived in the southern forest too. Dog asked to share a house with Eagle, and Eagle agreed. And so Dog climbed up into Eagle's nest. But at night, Dog started barking and Eagle told him to stop: bad things roamed in the dark.

"Dog thought to himself that Eagle was proud but cowardly at night, and so Dog set off to find a braver friend. Also in the forest, he found Owl, who also lived high in the trees. Owl wasn't scared of the dark. But when Dog barked in the daytime, Owl told him to stop: Fox might hear them."

Syra felt ridiculous prattling off this children's story to an adult man, but he had asked for it. She continued the story: Dog lived with other animals, but found each too cowardly for his liking. So Dog continued wandering until he found Human, who was not scared of anything. And Dog lived with Human still.

"That is an interesting choice of animals," Viktor said. "Eagle, Owl, Fox, Wolf, Seal."

"They're sacred animals," Syra said. "There's the Deer, too."

"But Dog didn't live with them?" he asked.

She shook her head. "Deer was dead by then."

Viktor didn't ask any more questions after that – which was fine by Syra – and so they walked several more miles until the forest thinned, giving way to a broad but shallow river.

While her companion filled his waterskin, Syra forded the river to scrape reindeer moss from a boulder on the far side. It was not a particularly tasty or nutritive food, but it would fill her belly. Scooping water into her soapstone bowl, she climbed the bank and then started a small fire, over which she boiled the moss. Crossing the river, Viktor found his own place to sit a dozen or so feet away from her. Using a twig to stir her strange concoction, she silently acknowledged the moment of privacy.

Again, her stomach knotted. She had never been away from her family for more than two days. She had been gone five days now. Not only was she homesick, but she worried about her mother's persistent cough, her siblings' ability to fish and trap without her help, her father's reluctance to sell the wares that he carved, and her newborn nephew surviving until summer. She scrubbed at her stinging eyes.

Her water boiled over.

The contents of her bowl were nothing more than dark mush, but it meant the moss was edible. Rummaging in her pack for her spoon, she glanced at Viktor, who stared emptily at the river.

Syra grunted and, taking her bowl, strode over to the Ruthenian.

"There's enough for two," she said.

His gaze climbed slowly from her boots to her face. "I didn't ask you to cook for me."

Syra folded her legs and sat. "I cooked for myself."

"Still." His eyes were the color of hardening sap, the midday light catching on flecks of brown and orange. For a moment, Syra wanted to know what he was thinking. "Thank you."

"Eat," she said. "It doesn't taste good, but it's something."

Viktor didn't speak as he ate, his movements efficient and economizing. He reminded Syra a bit of a stray dog. An unfamiliar pang touched her heart before she shook herself and swallowed down the bitter-tasting moss. She didn't need to imagine him as anything but the man who had taken her away from her family.

CHAPTER 5

Bereza

On the seventh day of travel, they reached Bereza, which lay on the very edge of Ruthenia. Though the hamlet fell within the princedom of Rodgorod, Viktor doubted the three families here paid taxes or *barshchina* to any lord. Sitting in front of her unpainted cottage, the ten-year-old girl Tsilia Aronovich spotted him and Syra and hollered for her father, the headman.

"You look worse for the wear, my friend." The portly and balding Aron Iosifevich shook Viktor's hand.

"I gave my supplies to the Sarnoks," Viktor explained. "They had a hard winter."

"It was a cold one." Aron jerked his chin towards Syra. "Looks like you brought a companion."

Viktor turned to introduce her. "This is–"

"Syra," she said.

"I didn't know Sarnoks left their tundra," Aron said to Viktor.

"Doesn't your Princess have an alliance with the Storm Owl clan?" Syra asked in flawless Ruthenian. "Their Pathfinder had to travel all the way to your white city to make it."

The headman had the decency to blush. "I'm sorry, miss, I didn't realize you spoke our language."

Syra shrugged. "We trade with Ruthenians sometimes."

Viktor was a fool. He hadn't even considered that Syra would know Ruthenian. He had spent months in Beluvod, learning Sarnok vocabulary and grammar from Parmian merchants so that he could communicate with the tundra clans.

He hadn't even considered that Syra might know *his* language. He would wager that she spoke Parmian as well, meaning she was as well-educated in languages as he was. Just in different languages. And she had a practical reason for it. He was just a *boyar*'s son, educated for the sake of it.

"Well, I hope you forgive my rudeness," the headman said. "I am Aron Iosifovich, and welcome to Bereza. We do not have much here, but we would be happy to share a meal and our *banya* with you."

"I'll take the meal," Syra said.

"Their *banya* is simple," Viktor said, "but we both need it."

She frowned at him. "Why would I need this … *banya*?"

Oh. Viktor fidgeted with the handle of his belt knife. She didn't know that word. "A *banya* is a room that holds steam. It relaxes your muscles and helps your blood flow. There can be pools, too, for bathing."

"You don't scrub yourself with soap and snow?" She arched her eyebrows at the two men and then shook her head. "Interesting."

Just like Viktor's last visit, Aron invited his guests to stay in his own home. Sensing that he was not the person to initiate her into Ruthenian *banyas*, Viktor sent Syra with Aron's wife, Raisa, while he and the headman shared pine nuts and birch-flavored *kvass*. When the women returned, it was Viktor's turn in the sauna. And then he and Syra shared a supper of cabbage soup and nut bread with the family.

They ended supper with heated *kvass* and then retired to bed – Aron and his family to the second room, Viktor and Syra to their bedrolls in front of the hearth. As always, the Sarnok woman pointedly faced away from him.

This time, Viktor laid on his side, his head propped up on his arm, for a long moment. The firelight glistened in her braid, threads of blue-black and firebird-red. When his thoughts turned indecorous, he turned over. He didn't need to wonder about what she might look like beneath the coat and her coveralls. Or what her skin might feel like against his. Syra barely deigned to speak to him. She would probably disembowel him if she ever caught him looking *that* way.

He was here because his father wanted magic to control the *leshy*. The Bone Doll did that. Viktor wasn't here to involve himself with the woman who owned the damn thing.

The ceiling beams formed multi-point stars above his head, like a false wooden sky. And to his right, Syra twisted and turned in her bedroll, sniffling softly. Fisting the fabric of his bedroll, Viktor tried to stop himself. She didn't want his help. She would brush him off like she always did. But her distress made his teeth ache.

And so, he wriggled closer and set his hand on her shoulder. "What is wrong?"

"I miss home."

And if I had not come for the Bone Doll... "It won't be very long," he lied. "And then you'll be back home."

Syra turned onto her back. She was not facing him, but she wasn't facing away either. "How long will your lord keep me there, in Zoldrovya?"

For a long, long time. But he couldn't say that, not when she wanted to return home so badly. "I don't know."

She took a shuddering breath and folded her arms around herself, staring at the ceiling with wet eyes. A terrible pain throbbed through Viktor's jaw and into his skull. He hated a woman in distress, and somehow it was a hundredfold worse when *he* was the source of it all.

"You need to rest," he said because he had nothing else. "We have a long way to go." Still, red ringed her eyes and she sniffled. So Viktor tried something else. "My nursemaid used to tell me stories when I could not sleep. Let me tell you one."

Syra's gaze slid to him, skeptical.

Viktor took that as assent and began. "In a certain princedom, in a certain time, there lived a great warrior named Dobrynya. He traveled the princedom, saving villages from greedy *zmey* who stole gold and livestock. One day, he arrived in the Prince's city, and the Prince called him into attendance. The

Prince's daughter had been taken by Zmey Izumrudovich – an emerald-scaled dragon known for its hunt for the most beautiful jewels in the world – and the Prince, knowing Dobrynya's prowess, demanded that the warrior rescue his daughter."

In soft tones, Viktor told Syra how Dobrynya sought out each Ruthenian god, lamenting that he did not have the weapons to defeat a *zmey* like Izumrudovich. Rodú, the God of Fate, offered the warrior a mirror made of glass; Zorya, the Goddess of War, a spear made of hawthorn; Devana, the Goddess of the Hunt, a swift horse; and Veles, the God of the Dead, told him to pray. Thus armed by the gods, Dobrynya set off to fight the *zmey*. The former three gifts helped Dobrynya fight the *zmey*.

"But Izumrudovich was strong," continued Viktor, "and so the warrior fought him for three days. By the fourth day, Dobrynya was failing and so he said his prayers to Veles. The god told him to fight for four more hours. And so Dobrynya did. And he defeated the *zmey* at the fourth hour on the fourth day. With his spear, he split open the ground and sent Zmey Izumrudovich deep into the earth, never to be seen again. And thus, the Prince's daughter was rescued.

"The Prince offered his daughter in marriage to Dobrynya, but the warrior declined. He was a peasant and could not marry her, so instead Dobrynya gave her to the Grand Prince to be his bride."

During the tale, Syra had turned to him. "Do Ruthenian men always give up their prizes?"

"Only the noblest."

Viktor rested his head in the crook of his arm, watching her eyelids flutter closed. As her breathing deepened and steadied, he rolled onto his back. His chest hurt in a good way; and he fell asleep remembering all the stories he had loved as a boy.

CHAPTER 6
The Thaw

South and east of Bereza, the narrow road passed through thick and wild forest. Fortunately, the oppressiveness of the forest was lightened by Syra's thawing. Viktor wouldn't call their relationship congenial, but their silences no longer felt like the depths of winter; and Syra answered more easily when he asked her a question. Daily, Viktor breathed a sigh of relief that his traveling companion didn't hate him. Or not as much as she had. It made traveling decidedly more comfortable, though it did cause him to catch himself admiring her starling-black hair and warm brown skin a bit too frequently. Viktor knew she wouldn't appreciate his ogling.

On the tenth day of their journey, they came to a fork in the road.

"What's the matter?" Syra asked.

"I'm just trying to read these." He squinted at the weather-worn waystones. One said *Bel–* and the other *Belu–*. As if *both* paths went to the city by the lake. No matter how hard he tried to read the other letters, he couldn't make them out.

"Which way did you come from?"

Neither, if he was being honest. Viktor didn't remember this fork in the road. He had taken a straight, uninterrupted shot from Beluvod to Bereza and then the tundra. He scratched at his hairline, glancing between the two waystones. Well, he couldn't stand here forever.

"That way," he decided, jerking his chin to the southwesterly path.

Syra hesitated, her hand twitching towards the waystones

minutely before she closed it into a fist. "Are you sure?"

"Yes, of course," he said with all the confidence he could muster.

"I feel like–"

"Beluvod and Zoldrovya are southwest of here," he said. "That path goes southwest. It must be that path."

"Okay." She gestured flatly for him to lead the way.

Viktor forced a smile to reaffirm to Syra – and himself – that *of course* he knew the way. He didn't want her to think he was incompetent or so forgetful that he didn't know how to get back home. It was easy: just head southwest. He would recognize the trail soon enough, and Syra would never be the wiser.

However, as he guided her down the trail, he didn't see any familiar landmarks. His hands began to sweat inside his gloves.

He tried to distract himself. "You said your grandfather made the Bone Doll. He was a shaman, yes? What I wanted to ask is: what do Sarnok shamans like your grandfather do? They have magic, it seems. They can make these … talismans."

Her lips pressed into a fine line, and for a moment, Viktor worried he might have hit a sore subject. But then her expression eased and she said, "Our shamans deal in one of the three worlds – the sky, the earth, or the underworld. My grandfather was a *vidutana*, meaning he was a sky shaman."

"Did he teach you any of his magic?" Viktor asked.

Syra shrugged. "I'm a *vidutana* as well, but I don't have magic like him. I can't even read omens in the stars. I can't make my soul leave my body and I definitely cannot make a talisman like the Bone Doll. Only the most powerful can do that."

Viktor recognized the shame in her voice. He had it too, buried deep inside. His father had wanted a strong and violent son. Instead, Igor Sviatopolkovich got Viktor, a coward and a liar. "It can be hard when we don't live up to expectations."

"No one expects me to be a sky walker," she said. "But it would have been nice to at least prophesy."

He admitted silently that prophesying might have helped him pick the right path. Because he *still* didn't recognize the thin trees with bluish-green needles that surrounded them, nor the stretch of yellow-brown grass ahead.

"I'm sure you know lots of stories, though," he said to change the subject. "Holy people are a font of stories."

She gave a noncommittal grunt.

"Perhaps you can tell me one of your grandfather's stories," he said. "Even a true one. I've never heard of a man who could walk in the sky."

She eyed him sidelong and said instead, "Something's rotting."

"It's just the thaw," he insisted as the trees gave way to waterlogged grass and large spans of yellow mud. "Dead leaves being exposed after a long winter, and all."

"The spring melt can make low-lying areas dangerous," she said. "It turns solid ground into a mire."

"The road is still raised here." He gestured. "If we stay on it, we'll avoid the mud and any quagmires there might be."

Syra wrinkled her nose but said nothing else.

Viktor adjusted the straps of his pack as he led onward. He wasn't a pampered lordling anymore. He had been traveling for two years. He knew how to handle bad roads. And here, he could show Syra how capable he was.

The path narrowed as the patches of mud and snowy slush widened. Gnats swarmed, and he batted them away from his face. Ahead, trees and more solid ground awaited. This muddy field wasn't *that* large. They'd be out of here in no time. And the road was fine, just slick.

He glanced back. Syra slogged after him with one hand over her abdomen – right over where the Bone Doll lay. As though it were a child in her belly and not an old piece of carved bone. The mud oozed over his boots, sucking him downward as he paused.

He saw it happen.

The path beneath Syra's feet collapsed in a rush of slush and water. Syra buckled and tumbled into the quicksand below. His heart in his throat, he clambered in and reached for her. The quicksand snatched his legs; and Viktor floundered. Fetid gas bubbled up around them, busting with sickening fumes. Gagging, Viktor grabbed Syra's arms and pulled. But it only made him sink deeper in.

She shoved him away. Wrenching her belt knife from the mud, she hacked at her pack's straps until the pack snapped free and sunk beneath the quicksand. Then, half-crawling, half-swimming, she dragged herself back to the narrow strip of road.

"Get on your belly." Her voice was hoarse, her face flushed. "Make yourself flat, wide. You have to float."

Lowering himself into the mud and spreading his limbs, Viktor did as she instructed. Then, carefully, he wriggled forward on the fetid surface. When he was close enough, Syra grabbed his pack and hauled him onto higher ground.

On his hands and knees, covered in mud, Viktor gasped for air. Syra stared down at him as though he were nothing more than a snake she had encountered on the road. He lowered his head. He wanted to hide. One wrong turn and he had nearly gotten them killed. And jumping in after her had done absolutely nothing. *She* had saved *him*. So much for being a capable traveling companion.

He dropped his gaze. "Thank you."

Though he knew that Syra dealt in silence, he still expected her to yell, to scold, to mock. His father, his mother, his tutors, and even the few people he considered friends used their words to cut him when he made a fool of himself like this.

But Syra said nothing, simply turning back to the path and walking on. Trying futilely to shake the mud off his clothes, Viktor stood and then followed her. And if he couldn't be more miserable, a breeze descended from the north, making his damp clothes heavy and cold. He let her lead for now so she couldn't see him. This was always what happened when he tried to be heroic.

His boots sloshing along the waterlogged path, Viktor remembered being the age of six or seven and watching the older boys training with an obstacle course, under the armsmaster's dictatorial eye. Viktor had wanted to be a great warrior like the knights in his fairytales; and so he brashly entered the obstacle course one night after training. He ended up falling from a rolling log and broke both legs. He was only discovered by the armsmaster the next morning. The arms master had ridiculed him for thinking he – a "little boy" – could finish an obstacle course that challenged battle-hardened soldiers. And Viktor's father had beaten him raw, broken bones and all, for being such an embarrassment.

He never had walked quite right since, though he did his best to hide it.

Viktor scrubbed at his face, the dried mud turning to grit beneath his palm. He wished Syra would say *something*. The worst insult couldn't be as bad as this disappointed silence. But she wasn't like anyone else he had ever known. Faced with his utter insufficiency, she simply ignored him. Which only reminded Viktor more clearly how he had tried to impress her, but instead *she* had to drag him out of a mess of his own making.

Turning towards Syra, Viktor opened his mouth to speak and then stopped. What use were words when he could have gotten her killed?

CHAPTER 7

Cherry Trees

Bereza had seemed very much like a Ruthenian version of a Sarnok campsite – a cluster of families living in small homes, made from rushes and sticks rather than reindeer skin. But Syra couldn't quite wrap her mind around this Ruthenian town. Yes, the homes were small, but they were made from stone – not portable in the slightest. And the roads were tiled, making Syra feel as though she was walking on a floating platform.

"This is Vishnaya. It's named after the cherry trees." Viktor pointed at one of the many trees lining the roads. It bloomed *pink*, not green. "I stayed at the Bloom and Bramble Inn when I was here last. It has decent accommodations."

Following him down a different road, Syra scowled at the strange trees and then at the market stalls lining the road. Was this what Ruthenia looked like – pink trees, stone buildings, and streets crammed with merchants? It felt like a totally different world from the one she lived it.

"This is it," he announced.

Syra said nothing as she stepped inside the establishment. Viktor did seem to enjoy the sound of his own voice. His voice wasn't unpleasant. But it was odd that he would talk, even if she didn't respond.

Inside were several long wooden tables and accompanying benches, where Ruthenians sat drinking, eating, and gambling. Syra felt their gazes turn to her and a flicker of frustration lit in her chest. She probably looked like some frightening mud creature after thrashing around in that quicksand. Viktor certainly did.

As Viktor spoke with the innkeeper, Syra reached inside her coat and wrapped her fingers around the Bone Doll. It was warm to the touch, like a living thing. After the death of her grandfather last summer, it had become a curse, luring children and reindeer away. A painful, prickling chill crawled up her spine. Had it led Viktor down the wrong path? They could have died.

When he was finished talking to the proprietor, Viktor turned to her with that stiff smile that Syra found unsettling. "We have two rooms across the hall from each other on the second floor."

She didn't know what rooms at an inn looked like – she had spent her entire life in her family's *mya* – but she said, "A covered place to sleep will be nice."

His smile grew more brittle. "Vishnaya also has a *banya*, just behind the inn. We'll both feel better once we get this mud off us."

And so, Syra left the Bloom and Bramble to find the *banya* just west of the inn. Unlike Bereza's, this one was indoors and resembled all the other buildings in town – a stone structure with a tiled roof. And on one end was a door with a painting of a woman, the other end had a matching painting of a man. Taking the door with the woman, Syra entered, stripped in the front room, and then moved deeper into the dimly-lit *banya*. The second room was dark and full of steam, with brightly-burning coals sitting in the center of a room. Dark shadows – other women – moved from time to time, splashing water onto the coals and creating a thicker mist. Finding a bench along the wall, Syra listened to the women talk and laugh amongst themselves. She poured warm water along her limbs and scrubbed them with the birch branches left in every corner. And slowly, the tension in her muscles eased and she relaxed against the stone wall, her eyes slipping closed. For a moment, she pretended she was in the dark warmth of her *mya*, her siblings whispering around her.

Then, somewhere to her right, a woman with a deep voice said something about "the newcomer with the red hair."

"I wonder if he's red *all the way down*," said another.

"Mm, it would be delicious to find out," the deep-voiced

woman replied.

Syra pressed her back against the stone wall, an unfamiliar feeling snaking through her chest. Viktor was... Well, she had never seen a man with orange hair before. And his amber eyes were always bright, like a bird of prey's. Neither orange hair or amber eyes seemed particularly rare in Ruthenia, but she guessed that these women weren't the first who had been interested in Viktor.

Syra was just surprised that she ... agreed? ... with the women.

Not about wanting to find out anything "delicious" about him. Or find any more orange hairs. But he was nice enough to look at. She shook herself. She must be tired if she was thinking things like that about a Ruthenian.

"I wonder why he's with that tundra woman," the second said.

"Likely guarding her," said the first. "A gentlemanly knight escorting a lady."

"Do the tundra people *have* ladies?"

Syra's jaw tightened. The Sarnok didn't have nobility. They didn't need them. So why did those Ruthenian people say it like the Sarnoks *lacked* something fundamental? Careful not to move too quickly, she stood and clung to the wall as she moved to the exit. Syra didn't really know what a knight was, but she did not like the insinuation that the Sarnok were unworthy of protection or guidance.

She was too tired to listen to those women.

She left the *banya*, grimacing as she dressed in her still-muddy clothes. Then, she reached into her pocket, her fingers tightening around the Bone Doll. A faint, warm pulse traveled through her palm and up her forearm. Almost as though it was comforting her. She let the figurine go.

She found Viktor waiting at the inn. A mug of the Ruthenian drink, *kvass*, and a bowl of soup waited for her; Viktor had empties. He flipped and caught a copper coin idly. "You look better."

"You're still filthy," she said.

"I needed to make sure you were fed," he replied.

Gratitude flickered inside Syra, but she snuffed it out. She had already admitted to herself that he *might* be nice to look at. She didn't need to start liking him. He was the reason she was homesick. She found something else to think about.

"What is a knight?"

"A knight?" He blinked. "A man who fights for his lord. But it's more than a soldier. He's noble usually, though not always, and has a moral code to which he abides."

Syra tilted her head. *A gentlemanly knight escorting a lady.* Was Viktor a warrior? A nobleman warrior? She had cared more that Viktor had dragged her away from her family than she did about *who* he was. She didn't know much of anything about him. "What sort of moral code?"

"Knights should be brave, loyal, honest, generous, and devout," he said.

"They are like your Dobrynya," she concluded.

"Yes." Color bloomed in his cheeks as though she had caught him in a lie. "Dobrynya was a knight. I … didn't think you knew the word."

"But he was not noble," Syra said. "He could not marry his princess."

Viktor pinched the coin, digging his nail into its face. "He was born a serf and then made a knight after helping another knight, called Lyoshenka."

"What did Dobrynya help this Lyoshenka with?" Syra asked. *What makes a man noble enough to become a knight?*

Viktor set the coin on the table, his posture relaxing as though even the thought of a story set him at ease. Or perhaps Syra had steered away from whatever had made him blush. "In a certain princedom, in a certain time, there lived a knight named Lyoshenka, who worked in service for the Grand Prince. One day, the Leshy Prince came to court. Being a wild spirit from the forest, the Leshy Prince showed no manners: it ate all the food, drank all the wine, and insulted the Grand Prince in his home. Offended on his lord's behalf, Lyoshenka mocked the Leshy Prince, saying he was an overfed cow.

"The Leshy Prince grew very angry at the insult and told Lyoshenka that in four years, four months, and four days, the Leshy Prince would return and bury Lyoshenka alive. Lyoshenka laughed it off, and the Leshy Prince rode away. But as the years, months, and days passed, Lyoshenka began to worry: what if the Leshy Prince *did* return and *did* bury him?"

Viktor spun a tale of the arrogant knight growing more and more paranoid, seeking new ways to protect himself from the forest creature. He prayed to the gods, lay a ring of salt around his house, burned torches at all hours, and even began building a moat. But still time moved forward; and Lyoshenka knew the Leshy Prince was coming.

"And finally, the *leshy* arrived. He stepped across the moat and salt, knocked aside the torches, and went straight for Lyoshenka," Viktor continued. "They fought all day and all night, breaking their swords in their efforts and so they had to wrestle with bare hands in the end. By daybreak, it looked very much like the Leshy Prince would bury Lyoshenka in the earth. But then a serf appeared. His name was Dobrynya, and he carried his woodsman's hatchet. With four perfect strikes, he removed the *leshy*'s head.

"As a reward for slaying the *leshy*, the Grand Prince bestowed knighthood on Dobrynya," Viktor finished. "And for defending his honor to the death, the Grand Prince gave his daughter to Lyoshenka to marry."

"Lyoshenka didn't *do* anything," Syra protested. "Why did he marry the daughter?"

"I just said: he defended the Grand Prince's honor."

"No, he insulted the Leshy Prince," she said. "Everyone knows not to insult spirits – or they might come after you."

Viktor turned red again, dragging the copper coin across the table top. He looked … fetching … with flushed cheeks. "He's one of the heroes. Something good had to happen to him, or the story would be sad."

She shook her head. "That's a terrible story: you don't learn anything from it."

"You learn to be brave and strong. And not give up hope when things get desperate."

Syra opened her mouth to speak and then stopped herself. His color high, he was breathing hard – as though he were about to burst. She didn't *like* him, but she didn't want to fight with him. She took a gulp of *kvass* to regroup. "Maybe I just didn't understand your story," she said half-heartedly.

"Knights are *honorable*," Viktor insisted. "They struggle, but they are good in the end."

Syra frowned. Was he talking about Lyoshenka and Dobrynya anymore? Maybe she didn't want to know. She was here to help him with a *leshy*. She didn't need to know more about him. She dropped her gaze to her soup, signaling that she was done with this conversation. Viktor sighed, but Syra refused to acknowledge him.

CHAPTER 8
The World Unbalanced

Syra was certain she hated *nothing* more than she hated Ruthenian rain. Yes, it rained on the tundra, but nothing like this. This was a deluge. Even protected by the trees, she felt like she was walking through a waterfall. Her reindeer hide clothes were heavy; and anything they didn't cover was soaked. Underfoot, the road grew muddy and slick; and she wondered if they wouldn't find quicksand soon.

Stuffing her hand into her coat, she gripped the Bone Doll. It was hot and dry. What she wouldn't give to be back in her *mya* and on the tundra, out of this mess.

Then, from the corner of her eye, she spotted it. It was little more than a few wooden boards leaned together with dead leaves piled atop, but it was a shelter very similar to what Sarnok hunters made when making multi-day treks. Making an incoherent noise at Viktor, she jogged towards the lean-to. Water streamed through a hole in the corner, but all-in-all, it was drier than outside. She crawled inside, and Viktor followed.

"I can't believe you spotted this," he said.

Syra sucked her teeth. The space was *very* tight with two people. She was almost nose-to-nose with Viktor. And was that him that smelled like cinnamon? She shifted as far back as she could.

"There's not much room," he said, stating the obvious. "Let me help you get your pack off."

Before she could tell him that she didn't need his help, he was pulling the straps off. And even that small brush of his fingers made her throat constrict. She let him remove the straps from her arms. The pack slumped onto the ground behind her.

Doing everything she could not to touch Viktor, Syra turned to her pack and then groaned. Unlike her old reindeer hide pack, this one was made of wool and wasn't waterproof. Everything was soaked. Including her bedroll. Her hands began to tremble. In the tundra, a wet bedroll could mean death by hypothermia, even in the summer months if the temperatures dipped low enough.

Viktor was rummaging behind her. And when she glanced over her shoulder, she saw him unfurl his *dry* bedroll. She clenched her fists. She told herself that the world wasn't conspiring against her. It was just bad luck. In her pocket, the Bone Doll twitched. She turned away.

She wished she was home.

She must have looked miserable because Viktor said, "You can take my bedroll."

"My clothes are warm enough." A cold gust rattled the shack. Syra sighed. It was going to be a long night.

She stiffened at the weight of his hand on her shoulder, an uncomfortable, liquid-like emotion pooling in her chest. Her fingers tightened around the Bone Doll, still secure in her pocket.

"I can't let you sleep on the wet ground."

She craned her neck to look at him. He was pale, his orangebush-colored hair plastered to his skull. He looked as miserable as she felt. "You'll freeze to death in just your sodden woolens."

"I can keep warm," he said unconvincingly.

Syra winced. He sounded pathetic. But she probably sounded the same, trying to avoid using his bedroll. "Fine," she acquiesced. "But only if you share it. I won't have you dying of hypothermia before you can take me back home."

Viktor turned red to the tips of his ears, but he nodded. "Fine."

"And *do not* touch me," she warned, jerking her shoulder out of his grasp. "And don't look either."

His expression grave, he nodded.

Stripping off her coat and boots, Syra went first into the

bedroll, covering herself with the top layer and turning her back to Viktor. For several moments, she waited, listening to him rustle about. But curiosity and impatience got the better of her. She peeked over her shoulder.

His back to her, the Ruthenian had removed his cloak and now was shrugging out of his caftan. Beneath, he wore a tunic with fine pleats. The thin and wet fabric clung to his shoulders. Hastily, he pulled the tunic off, revealing wiry muscle and skin that was unscarred by hunting accidents or even the simplest hazards Syra saw on the tundra. She had never seen skin so smooth. A coil deep and low inside her tightened.

Syra turned away, hugging herself. She shouldn't have looked.

Now, when he squeezed into the bedroll beside her, his back facing hers, her skin tingled. She told herself she was a fool and he was the cause of all this trouble. But that didn't stop the dark, hot feeling inside her belly.

"You're stiff," Viktor said.

Well, she hadn't intended to share a bedroll with the man who had pulled her away from her family and into the Ruthenian wilderness. "I'm cold."

"I told you about Lyoshenka yesterday," he said. "Let me tell you about *leshys*."

She was quiet. She hadn't asked about the spirit she was meant to bind. She just assumed she would fail. She couldn't read omens. How did anyone expect her to bind this angry forest spirit back to its trees? But maybe with the Bone Doll, she could dispel it like she had that strange red spirit.

"Sometimes, *leshys* look like humans., but there's always something wrong with them. They'll have no eyelashes or they will button their caftans wrong," Viktor said. "Other times they'll look like men made from trees with gnarled, bark-like skin. And they're always tall. They usually like to run with and hunt the forest creatures, and the worst they'll do is lead travelers off the path.

"Zoldrovya's *leshy* used to be like that," he continued. "You used to not know there *was* a *leshy*. But about 10 years ago, it began to overtake the estate. It lured children away from their families, never to be seen again. It strangled livestock in the night. And now it's trying to tear the manor down."

The Bone Doll hummed against her belly, low and subtle like a cold breeze. Syra bit her lip. The *leshy* and her grandfather's figurine sounded eerily similar.

"They should have sent you with a stronger *vidutana*," she said. "I can't even protect my own clan from that sort of thing."

She felt Viktor stiffen. "You can't do it?"

"I told you: I don't have much magic."

"But the Bone Doll does."

"Yes," she said hesitantly.

"I know you can." His voice was barely audible. "You have to."

Syra said nothing more, and soon Viktor began to breathe heavier, sleeping. She let her eyes drift shut even as her fingers ached from gripping the doll. And Syra slept, for a time.

Then the Bone Doll spoke.

Its voice was a rattle, like rabbit bones tossed in the wind. Its voice was a whistle, the summer wind in the grass. Its voice was her grandfather's, chanting to their ancestors. It spoke only in fragments and in words Syra didn't understand. It was inside her head, whispering, whispering, whispering. And then it screamed.

Images flashed in her mind. Men with axes. Branches crushing bone. Leaves rustling. Women digging. Blood trickling along roots. Children humming. The forest turning black.

Gasping, Syra sat upright.

The starlight filtering through the branches was harsh, casting stark shadows on the earth. Above, only two of the Three Dogs were visible. *The world unbalanced,* she knew instinctively, the prophecy easy and simple for the first time in her life. She clung to that feeling.

Viktor was beside her, upright as well, with his belt knife in his hand. The starlight made his skin look smooth as sealskin. Syra dragged her gaze away. After a moment, Viktor lowered the blade, his expression softening. "Are you all right?"

They were in the lean-to, surrounded by damp leaves. The rain had, blessedly, stopped. The forest was dark, but not dead. No men with axes or women with shovels, nor bloodthirsty trees. Syra wiped the steaming sweat off her brow. "It was just a nightmare."

"It's that thing."

At some point while she slept, Syra had pulled the Bone Doll from her pocket. Now, it lay atop their bedroll like a lapdog, glowing faintly blue and twitching as though dreaming its own dreams. She swallowed against a wave of nausea. Were these the sorts of nightmares it gave the children it tried to lure away? The visions it gave the reindeer to induce them into a stampede? She snatched up the figurine and shoved it in her pocket.

"We should have left it buried," she said. "It's too dangerous."

Viktor lifted his hand as though to touch the doll in its pocket, but he stopped himself. "Is it hurting you?"

"No." Syra froze. She should pull away so he couldn't touch the Bone Doll. Yet her belly fluttered at how close they were. He was shirtless and … they had never touched skin to skin. "It was just a nightmare."

Viktor set his hands on the blanket purposefully as though he, too, was trying to stop himself from touching her. "Lie back down. I'll tell you another story."

Turning to face away from him, Syra lay back down and squeezed her eyes shut. The Bone Doll twitched and muttered, but she barely noticed. Instead, all she could think about was how warm the bedroll was – and how *touchable* Viktor had looked.

CHAPTER 9
Kholm

"This is Kholm," Viktor explained as they climbed the steep and rocky path up to the town built on the outcropping that overlooked the Snezhana River. "It's an outpost for the city of Beluvod."

At the palisades, the guards checked Viktor and Syra over, rummaging through their packs as well. Fortunately, they didn't ask why Syra was hugging her abdomen. He didn't know what she would do if she had to show her Bone Doll to Ruthenian soldiers. She didn't even like Viktor looking too closely at it.

When the guards let them pass, he made sure to look anywhere but Syra. Last night, in that damp shelter... He shouldn't have looked at her. She had even told him not to. Now, he was haunted by the memory of her perfectly sloped shoulder glimmering in the starlight. He swallowed. And no matter what he did, he was plagued by thoughts of kissing her soft throat.

She would *never* let him do that.

Made of the stone on which they sat, the buildings here were squat and rustic, but Kholm's residents were none the worse for it. Everyone wore finely spun wool, often printed with geometric patterns; and here and there, a woman wore a bolt of glossy silk imported from the east. Children played tag and hoop-diving in the streets, while the adults shopped at stalls selling everything from fine silver jewelry to luxuriant furs.

"The inn is this way." He jerked his chin to the east. "It's really just some cots in an old barracks, but–"

"Anything is better than where we were last night," Syra said.

Viktor grinned bitterly. Of course, she had hated being so close to him. Separate sleeping arrangements were much preferable. For her. His cheeks heated at the thought of sharing a bed with her, and he quickened his steps. Their ... predicament ... last night was as sexless as it could have possibly been. Syra had made it clear that she had wanted him to neither see nor touch her. It was his own damn fault that he had snuck a glance. Now he *knew* what he couldn't have.

Viktor acquired accommodations at the inn, and then he and Syra found the *banya*. While Syra lounged languidly in the steaming rooms, Viktor bathed and left quickly. He didn't need any more temptation.

Outside, the air was brisk and humid. Slicking his wet hair back, he headed back towards the barracks-turned-inn.

As he passed the town gates, he heard the sentries chatting.

"Did you see the foreign girl?" said the taller of the two.

"Aye, the one with the brown skin and wide eyes," his compatriot said. "Strange but pretty thing, she is. Like to wet my cock in her cunt."

Slowing to a stop, Viktor clenched his fists.

"I'd like to see her on her knees," the tall one said, "with those sweet little lips around my knocker."

The cords in his neck tightened painfully. But he forced himself to take a step and then another and another. He was no Lyoshenka or Dobrynya. He hadn't even completed arms training.

He couldn't fight those guards. And so he walked away, his anger turning into thick and oily shame.

He passed a vendor selling glass beads, much like the glass beads his mother and sisters wore. His shame grew heavier. They were four days from Zoldrovya, but he wished that it was longer. Viktor had been telling Syra that she needed to bind the *leshy* back to its forest – and then she could go home. But that wasn't the truth.

Igor Sviatopolkovich wanted a way to bend the *leshy* to his will. When Viktor had thought he was simply fetching an artifact, he hadn't cared at all about what his father wanted to use it for.

But now that Syra was involved... He couldn't tell her. What would she do if she knew he had lied? And Viktor could only imagine what his father would do if he jeopardized Igor's hopes to defeat and control the *leshy*. Viktor started to wish for some terrible catastrophe to destroy the road or set them off course, so that Syra wouldn't fall into his father's hands.

Shaking his head minutely, he walked away from the glass beads.

When he arrived at the barracks-turned-inn, Syra was sitting cross-legged outside, combing her hair with her fingers. He barely had enough pride to look at her. "You should be careful. I don't think everyone is friendly." *And some of us lie.*

"I can take care of myself," Syra said.

Viktor clenched and unclenched his fists. He could not defend Syra's honor nor could he tell her the truth, so what use was he? He was just his father's crony.

"Life on the tundra is violent, inherently. Something as simple as traveling from one campsite to another can turn deadly because of a broken sled runner or frostbite." Parting her hair, she began braiding it. "We don't wish for violence, we endure it."

His shoulders sagging, Viktor rubbed at a mud fleck on his caftan. "You shouldn't have to endure it. Someone should keep you safe."

Her fingers midway through her braid, Syra looked up and their gazes met. Her eyes were perfectly black, like jet beads, glimmering with a mix of surprise and something Viktor could not identify. Her wide, downturned lips parted as though she wanted to say something – but she hesitated. He had the sudden and strong urge to step forward and kiss her.

Blinking hard, he forced himself to look away. "Forgive me. I sound patronizing."

Letting her braid fall apart, Syra stood. His breath caught in his chest. They were so close. "You want to be one of your great knights," she said. "But what is so bad about Viktor?"

He was a coward, a liar, and a lackey who had never succeeded in anything. One who had dragged an innocent woman across miles and miles of wilderness, not because of what *he* wanted but what his father demanded. And he did a shit job at that, too, leading her through quicksand and failing to protect her name. He picked at the fleck of mud on his caftan.

"I didn't mean anything by it," he continued apologizing dumbly. "I just meant you shouldn't be alone in this world."

Her posture eased, her features softening. "I'm not alone. I have my parents, my siblings, my nephew, my clan…"

And I took them all from you. Viktor nodded, letting his shoulders slump. *He* was the one who was alone. The one who wanted someone to protect, to hold. Syra didn't need him. She just wanted to go home.

"Once you've subdued the *leshy*, I'll take you home," he lied because he knew it was what she wanted to hear. And he wished then that he was someone else, someone good, so that he didn't have to lie to make her happy.

CHAPTER 10
Star Souls

Syra sat on a retaining wall, watching a puppeteer perform. She had never seen anything quite like it; and, though she didn't recognize the story, she was delighted by the puppets, which were made from multicolored paper and sticks and decorated with fabric and glass beads. The puppeteer played out a story of a knight who went to slay a giant but befriended him instead.

Viktor came to lean against the wall beside her, and she was a bit surprised to realize that she was no longer frustrated by his presence. When had that changed?

"That's the story of the knight Ilya and the giant Sviatagor," Viktor said. "It's one of my favorites."

"Do you have any stories without knights?" she asked.

"Plenty." He crossed one ankle over the other and folded his arms across his chest in an easy, relaxed pose. "But my favorites have knights."

The puppeteer finished with a flourish of streamers on sticks and a magnificent puppet in golden armor. Then, the crowd tossed coins into his hat. Viktor slipped forward to hand the man a silver coin before resuming his position against the retaining wall. His hair gleamed like copper in the fading light, and Syra found remembering how he had given her clan most of his supplies.

Viktor fidgeted with his belt purse. "I meant to give this to you earlier."

Syra frowned at the strand of beads that dangled from his fingers. The beads were fine and detailed, just like the bone, antler, and ivory jewelry the Sarnok wore. The Sarnok didn't use glass, so she was surprised at how much it looked like colored ice. It *was* beautiful. But that didn't explain why Viktor was showing it to her.

She squinted at the necklace and then him. "What is it?"

"Just something I found." In the gray-blue twilight, she could not tell if he blushed, but he did start smoothing the front of his caftan with his free hand. "I know you didn't want to come, and this hasn't been an easy journey. I thought maybe this would be something good. That came from Ruthenia."

Syra sucked on her lower lip. Part of her was touched. The other part insisted this wasn't what it seemed. "You don't need to bribe–"

"It's a gift." Viktor's voice grew more insistent. "It made me think of you. That's all. Will you take it?"

She remembered lying on the floor of Aron Iosifovich's home in Bereza, so homesick that she couldn't sleep. He had scooched closer, warming her, and told her the story of Dobrynya and the *zmey*, lulling her to sleep. He could be sweet. Maybe that was what this was: sweet.

Syra held out her hand.

Viktor looked at her expectantly and then cleared his throat. "May I put it on you?"

Syra nodded and felt a strange ache in her chest. Undoing the first button of her coat, she pushed back her hood and collar. Viktor slipped the beaded strand around her neck, tying it in the back. He was swift, and he was proper. But he did not wear his gloves, and even the slightest brush of his fingertips sent heat crackling across her skin.

Viktor stepped back and seemed to look at everything but Syra.

"It's ... not ugly," she said, letting the cool glass soothe her suddenly too-hot skin.

"Thanks," he said. "I tried to avoid the ugliest ones."

She had no gift for him – none that she had planned – so she thought quickly. Unbuttoning the rest of her coat, she slipped her hand into one of the interior pockets. There, she found a knife barely the length of her palm that her father had carved from bone. "Here."

He held a hand up, his palm facing her. "There's no need."

"I want you to have it," she said. "It is meant for gutting fish."

"Practical." He took it and turned it over in his hands, examining the workmanship. "I gut so many fish."

Her lips quirked, and she almost smiled. "I can tell."

Syra studied him then – his coppery hair, his amber eyes, the angle of his lips. She knew what he wanted to be. He wanted to be a great warrior who fought monsters. But what did she know about him? She knew almost nothing beyond that he worked for a lord who wanted her to use the Bone Doll. And for most of this journey, she hadn't cared to know more. But he could be generous and sweet, and perhaps she *should* know more. Just a little.

"When I have bound the spirit and have returned to the tundra," she asked, "will you go home?"

Viktor hooked his thumbs in his belt. "I prefer to stay on the road."

"Your family must want you to visit at least," she said.

He smiled bitterly. "I'm not sure they miss me."

"Of course, they do," she said. "I would miss my brother, if he was traveling most of the year."

"Your family must miss you," Viktor said quietly. "Have you ever been away from them?"

Syra swallowed against the lump that had formed in her throat. She would give almost anything to be back in her family's *mya*, sitting and chatting with her parents, playing with her baby nephew, bickering with her siblings. "They know I'll return."

They fell silent for several moments as the puppeteer packed up his materials and then left. The twilight faded into night, and no one else walked this road. But Viktor and Syra remained.

Viktor tilted his face towards the sky. "You said your grandfather could walk in the sky. What does that mean?"

Even with her weak magic, Syra felt the stars' pull as

though they wanted her close but could not reach her. The Sirtian Hunter's seven stars burned brightly tonight. Her grandfather said that the Sirtian Hunter always foretold magic, but the stars did not deign to tell Syra *what* magic they prophesied.

"A long time ago, there was only Sky, and people lived in the Sky," she said. "But when the Sky birthed the Earth, the people were split. Their souls were split: half of the soul lived on the Earth and half lived in the Sky. For a while, everyone could feel that they were sundered in two, but eventually that faded. But just because we cannot feel it doesn't change the fact that each star in the Sky is half a soul, a twin for someone on Earth. The *vidutana*, the Sarnok sky shamans, still have that connection to their sky-souls, and through that connection they have magic.

"Most *vidutana* can read the stars for omens and prophecies, but the strongest ones have other abilities. Some can manipulate moon- and starlight. Others can create powerful talismans like the Bone Doll. And still others can detach their souls from their bodies and let their souls wander amongst the stars. My grandfather could make talismans and he could detach his soul and travel into the sky to commune with our star-souls."

Viktor raised his eyebrows, still gazing at the sky. "So, somewhere up there is star-Viktor."

The possibility of Ruthenian star-souls had never crossed her mind, but she said, "Yes."

"I wonder what he is doing up there." His voice was distant. "I wonder if he has made something of himself."

"Perhaps he's wondering the same about you," she said.

Viktor turned to face her, still casually leaning against the retaining wall. "He would be sorely disappointed."

"Or perhaps he would be envious of all you've done."

Fidgeting with his belt purse, Viktor glanced down quickly and then back to her. "I have done very little."

"You have traveled from your home in the heart of Ruthenia all the way to the tundra. You have enough to pay for food and lodging. And you are kind. Some might consider you fortunate."

"Do you find me fortunate?" he asked.

"It doesn't matter what I…"

The words died on her tongue as he lifted her chin with a curved finger. "When I look at you, I see a woman who is strong and can survive anything; a woman who knows more about the wilderness than I ever will; a woman who knows magic; a woman who loves her family and her people."

Her mouth was painfully dry. She should have been nothing more than a job – deliver her and the Bone Doll to Zoldrovya. But instead he saw *her*. Not the woman with too little magic to continue her grandfather's legacy, with too little magic to protect her clan from the Bone Doll's curse – but *Syra*. Her chest tightened as she realized how terribly he must want to be seen, in the same way he had seen her.

"How do you find me, Syra? Fortunate? Well-traveled? Generous?"

"You aspire to be a good man, but you don't see that you already are." Heat emanated from where his finger rested beneath her chin. "You shared your food with me on the road, when you did not have to. You comforted me when I could not sleep. You shared your bedroll when mine was wet. These are the acts of a good man."

His gaze grew soft, and he trailed his finger along her jawline, turning Syra's stomach to knots. His skin was soft and rough, cool and warm all at once. Gently, he bowed his head forward. The starlight caught in his orange hair, shimmering like a crown. Syra felt like a star glimmering in the darkness.

Then, Viktor kissed her.

Her eyes fluttered close as a pleasant heat, like a summer breeze, swelled inside her. His hand slid to cup her cheek, his kiss still gentle but intent. Instinctively, she leaned into him, parting her lips. He tasted like cinnamon and yearning. She rested her hands against his chest, his heartbeat wild beneath her palms.

Then, he pulled back, staring down at her with his lips parted in surprise. "Syra, I…"

Her mouth burned from his kiss, even as her heart began to sink. "Why are you looking at me like that?" *Like you didn't mean to kiss me at all?*

"I shouldn't have done that," he muttered. "I let my emotions get the better of me."

"You didn't want to kiss me?" How did you *accidentally* kiss someone?

"No. I mean, yes. I mean–" Viktor held up his hands in defeat. "Yes, I want to kiss you. You're a beautiful woman. Of course, I would. But I'm here to bring you to Zoldrovya; and you're here to handle the *leshy*. That has nothing to do with kissing you, or whether you like me or I like you."

"Are you trying to be one of your knights?" Syra had the sudden desire to laugh. "You can escort me, and I can bind your forest spirit, *and* you can still kiss me."

"A man should offer a bride-price, a home, a steady income–"

She grinned at his prudish logic. "I am a Sarnok, and I will go back to the tundra once I am done with your *leshy*. I don't want a Ruthenian husband, so I don't need your dowry or house." She leaned in. "But I might want more kisses. If that is something you are offering."

Viktor stared at her wide-eyed for a long moment before stammering, "Kisses, yes."

He stepped in, placed his hands at her waist, and kissed her again. Settling her hands upon his shoulders, she let her body and mind melt into a warm and bright summer.

CHAPTER 11
Rusalka

Below Kholm flowed the Snezhana River, its water white with rapids. According to Viktor, the river flowed southeastward into a lake so grand that it looked like the sea. Syra would believe that when she saw it. Her current problem was crossing the river. Like the tundra's rivers, the Snezhana overflowed in spring; and its waters had flooded the nearest bridge, sending Syra and Viktor southward to find calmer waters.

Several miles downstream, the rapids eased into calm but deep waters.

"Last time I tried something foolhardy, we got stuck in quicksand," Viktor said. "We should find a ferry."

"Where is the nearest one?" The Bone Doll twitched violently in her pocket. Syra shivered but saw nothing, only forest and river. She clutched the doll.

"I know the town of Dorazdel has one," Viktor said, unaware of any danger. "That's another three miles. I'm not sure if any enterprising ferryman has established another crossing somewhere between here and there."

The Bone Doll had gone quiet. Maybe the danger had passed. Still, as they walked, Syra scanned the trees for anything out of the ordinary. But the birch and spruce revealed nothing beyond the occasional brown-colored bird or twittering squirrel.

Eventually convinced that there was nothing there, Syra let her gaze find Viktor. Last night… She hadn't realized how nice it would be to kiss him. She supposed she had already admitted he was attractive, but the actual *feel* of him – soft lips, lean muscle

– was exquisite. She fingered her glass necklace. If she could kiss him every night from now until she returned to the tundra, that might be decent enough payment for her. Though Munku would still demand the silver.

Viktor caught her looking and blushed. She smirked. He did look fine with a little red on his cheeks.

"Maybe we should stop," she said. They didn't *have* to kiss at only night, did they?

"I'm trying to keep a good pace." He met her gaze and then said, "Oh."

Syra was crossing the distance between them when she heard a giggle. An icy shiver crawled down her spine. She and Viktor turned.

A beautiful woman combed her knee-length, sunshine-colored hair, sitting alongside the river. She smiled invitingly at them as though they were old friends. "Young lovers in spring."

This time Syra's cheeks heated. She had thought they were alone.

"Where are you going?" The yellow-haired woman's voice had an airy, tinkling noise to it – like a harness bell. "I don't see many travelers on this road."

"To the ferry at Dorazdel," Viktor said.

"You need to cross the river?" the woman asked, her eyes growing wide with excitement. "I can help you."

Syra's heart thudded. A woman sitting on the riverbank with no one else around? The woman looked so very … normal … but Syra's stomach curled when she looked too closely at the woman.

Viktor gripped Syra's hand. "Thank you, but we will take the ferry at Dorazdel."

"But you are here already." The woman pointed to the other side. "And it's not so far to cross."

"We don't want to bother–"

"*I am trying to help you.*" The woman's face twisted with rage as she surged to her feet. Her nails were so long that they curled back on themselves, cracking at the edges. She stepped forward, her ankles twisting inhumanly beneath her. *"Let me help you."*

Syra unsheathed her knife and sliced into the woman's fingers, before she could think. Viktor was pulling her backwards, away from the woman – *thing* – and telling her to run. The creature's blonde hair turned green and dripping like kelp, her eyes turning to gaping sockets in her skull. On all fours like an animal, she charged them. Syra slashed again as she ran. The woman-creature wrapped her thin fingers around Syra's ankle. Syra fell. Her lip splitting, she tasted blood. Her knife flew from her fingers. She kicked at the woman-creature's head, but the monster only snarled and started dragging her towards the river.

All the while, the woman-creature cooed, *"It's not so far to cross. Let me help you. It's not so far to cross."*

Viktor was running back for her. Falling to his knees, he grabbed Syra's arms and pulled. But the woman-creature was stronger, and Syra slipped from his grasp inch by inch.

When she was only holding on by the tips of her fingers, she remembered the strange red spirit in the forest and how it had retreated from her grandfather's chant. As fast as she could, she recited the words in Sarnok:

The world is ash, our hearts are stone.
Go! Return to your rightful home.

The Bone Doll pulsed like a second heartbeat against her belly, and Syra felt a bloom of power as she chanted. When she blinked, she saw the constellations behind her eyelids.

And then the moment was gone.

The woman-creature screeched and dropped Syra's ankle.

Viktor pulled Syra to her feet, and they ran. Away from the river. Into the forest. They stopped only when they couldn't hear the woman-creature screaming, nor the rushing of the river.

Syra bent forward, her hands on her knees, gasping for air. "What was that?"

"A *rusalka*," Viktor said, holding onto a tree for support. "A water spirit that tries to drown people."

She shuddered. It wasn't unheard of for Sarnok hunters, taking their umiaks onto the Silver Sea, to be caught in sudden storms and drown. For a Sarnok, it was the worst way to die – cold, painful suffocation. And there was no hope of making it to the underworld if you drowned because the sea took your soul instead. She assumed this *rusalka* had meant to keep her soul, too.

"Are you all right?" Viktor stepped closer. "Did she hurt your ankle?"

She breathed deeply, trying to calm her racing pulse. "I'm fine."

"Your incantation, it scared off the *rusalka*." He cupped her face. "Can you do that for the *leshy*?"

"I-I don't know." She had never experienced power like she had just wielded. It wasn't hers, but the Bone Doll's. And she didn't understand why it helped her.

Slowly, he let her go, the absence of his touch leaving a deep ache inside her. A curl of his orangebush-colored hair fell in front of his eyes. When she reached up to brush it away, he caught her hand. "You saved us."

"I wasn't going to fall prey to that creature."

"I'm lucky you're so stubborn," he said with a twisted smile and then kissed her knuckles. "Now, let's head south again. We *do* need to find Dorazdel and that ferry."

Can't we stay in the forest? Just a little longer? Syra didn't voice what she felt. Instead, she nodded and gestured for Viktor to lead the way.

CHAPTER 12
Beluvod

Beluvod – meaning "white water," according to Viktor – held more people than Syra knew existed in the entire world. And if she thought that the people of Kholm were wealthy and well-fed, it was nothing compared to the Beluvodians in their velvet and silver, their hair braided into elaborate but elegant styles. And not only Ruthenians lived here. Syra saw Parmians, Karelians, and Skanians, as well as other peoples she did not recognize. The buildings here were multi-storey and made of stone and wood, elaborately carved and painted with scenes from nature.

Just like the gray building on whose stairs she stood as Viktor fumbled in his belt purse.

"...is Goldenhome," Viktor was saying. "The steward, Yefrem Danilovich, has been my friend for a long time."

He produced a small, rusted key which he pressed into the lock. Syra scowled. Who had unrestricted access to their friend's home? "I had expected an inn."

"This is the Lord of Zoldrovya's city residence." Viktor's cheeks turned pink, and it reminded her of how he turned that same color when he kissed her. She wondered if he might kiss her again today. She wouldn't complain. "It's more economical to stay here. And Yefrem is here."

"Your friend," she repeated.

Golden-hued wood covered the floor and walls. And luxuriant, warm-toned furniture with velvet upholstery lured Syra further into the house. Goldenhome, it was called.

"There is a sitting room there." Viktor set his pack on

the floor by a jewel-toned tapestry depicting a midnight-haired woman in a blue hunting dress with lithe, black dogs running at her feet. "Let me get our rooms ready."

Relieving herself of her pack, she went into the sitting room. More silver gilding and vibrant tapestries. Filthy from more than two weeks of traveling, Syra felt wrong sitting on the immaculate furniture. Hugging herself, she turned a full circle, unsure of what to do now.

She spotted a painting in the corner, propped up on a golden-wood table and set in a silver frame. A man and woman, both orange-haired and wearing fine blue velvet, sat in golden wood chairs. At the woman's feet sat a pair of toddler-age girls with large green eyes and soft coppery curls. And at the man's left hand was a boy of about seven or eight years with ruddy cheeks and a sour expression. Syra examined them each again as the eerie feeling of having met these people before.

"Who are you?"

Syra jumped. In the doorway was an elderly man, his shoulders stooped and his pale skin heavily wrinkled. *Yefrem,* she reminded herself, her heart racing. *Viktor's friend.* "I'm Syra. You must be Yefrem. Viktor told me you worked here."

"Did he?" The old man shuffled forward. "And where is Viktor?"

"Upstairs, preparing the rooms."

Yefrem snorted, then, and shook his head. "The boy should tell me before he comes." He raised an eyebrow. "You're not Ruthenian."

"I'm Sarnok," she said.

He raised his eyebrows. "You came all the way from the tundra. Viktor didn't say he was going that far."

The Bone Doll twitched in her pocket, and she clasped it. "I'm going to help the Lord of Zoldrovya with a *leshy*. Viktor is escorting me."

"I'm glad Viktor has found something meaningful." When Syra tilted her head, Yefrem explained, "Viktor has always been a good boy, but he has always struggled to find purpose. Escorting you is the best thing he's done in years."

"You have known him for a long time." Curiosity drew Syra closer to the old man. Viktor's fairytales, those were where Viktor sought a purpose. But fairytales were moralistic and abstract; they didn't fit real life. Did this man hold Viktor's secrets? "He wants to be a knight."

"Everyone wants to be the hero in their own story," Yefrem said. "But rather than slay monsters, he makes his own."

Syra wanted to ask what the old man meant, but Viktor appeared at the foot of the stairs. He grinned hesitantly at both of them, like a man introducing his new bride to his disappointed parents. Syra swallowed, her throat dry. They had enjoyed a few kisses underneath the stars. They were *not* intended. This was a dalliance. And there was no reason for him to look at her like that. Or for her stomach to flutter.

"I see you met Syra," Viktor said.

Yefrem harrumphed. "I thought it was mice scurrying upstairs, but it was just you making yourself welcome."

"I missed you, too, Yefrem," Viktor said. "Now, can I show Syra to her room? She has traveled quite a long distance."

"All right, boy." Yefrem gestured for her to go. "I eat supper early these days, so be in the kitchen in an hour. Or you'll be eating cold soup."

Syra glanced over her shoulder as she climbed the stairs after Viktor. The old man looked at Viktor like a doting grandfather. Perhaps Viktor was the son of a steward. That made her pulse quicken. Viktor wouldn't be opposed to hard work, then, which was needed on the tundra.

She stopped herself again. This was a *tryst.* A tryst only. He could be as lazy and soft as he wanted. It did not matter because she would be returning home after she was done. He would travel Ruthenia's roads. They would never see each other again. And that was as it should be.

CHAPTER 13

A Pretty Bauble

After a supper of soup brimming with omul and wood sorrel, Viktor stayed with Yefrem at the table in the servants' quarters while Syra retreated upstairs. The steward opened a bottle of birch juice, pouring them each a mug, before slumping deep in his chair. It reminded Viktor of the hundreds of other times Yefrem had poured him birch juice, when Viktor needed a quiet place to sit where his parents and tutors would not find him.

Yefrem tested the birch juice. "You never send a note or anything ahead to announce yourself like a decent lordling."

Viktor laughed. "I thought you were resigned to the fact that I'm quite an *indecent* lordling."

The steward snorted. "I really had given up on you."

"Had?" Viktor raised an eyebrow.

"I never thought I'd see you guarding a lady," Yefrem said. "It's almost genteel."

"The Sarnoks don't have nobility." Viktor hid his face with a sip from his mug. When Yefrem said it, this job sounded almost … chivalric. A knight escorting a lady. But Viktor was only doing this because his father demanded it. And his father only demanded he did shit jobs.

"It's not the blood that makes a lord or lady, boy, it's the soul," the steward said. "My Karolinka was born a serf, but she was a lady through and through."

Viktor remembered Yefrem's wife, Karolina Adrianovna, with her graying red hair and meaty hands. She was a terror in her kitchen but as fond of fairytales as Viktor was. She had told him many stories that his nursemaid had not. Karolina had passed two summers ago, while Lord Igor had Viktor collecting taxes from Zoldrovya's serfs. Viktor had traveled night and day to make it to Karolina's funeral pyre, but he had been too late. She was ash when he arrived.

"Boy, you look like you're carrying an iron yoke around your neck," Yefrem said.

Viktor shrugged.

What was he supposed to do? He had failed his parents. He had failed his tutors. He had failed Karolina, and in doing so, Yefrem. Now, he was leading Syra down a dead-end road. And yet he still kissed her. And he wanted to kiss her again and again. He wanted to do *more* than kiss her. All night and all day, he had been plagued with what he wanted to do to her, with her. But Viktor was a liar, a coward, a failure. She deserved better than him.

It was too much to carry.

"My father wants Syra for her magic," he said, cradling his head in his hands. "She thinks she'll go home after binding the *leshy* deep in the forest. But my father wants to control the *leshy*. He will demand she remain and control the *leshy* for him. He won't let her go home."

Yefrem nodded over his mug.

"Syra, she's... She's tough and proud and intelligent. And I'm certain she hated me at the beginning. Everything I tried to do, tried to be, she saw straight through. I hated it. I *do* hate it. But she's" – he struggled for the words – "*more*. Better. And she makes me want to be better, like her. But I'm walking her straight into the wolf's jaws."

Yefrem sighed. "You've always wanted to be a hero, but you think it means swinging a sword and riding magical horses. That's only in the stories, boy. Real heroes are made of blood and scars and wounds so deep you cannot see them. You want to be good? Do right by the girl. Not what your father wants. Not what you want. *Her*. And perhaps she will return home and tell her family of the man who upheld his promises and set her free."

Viktor rubbed his forehead with his thumbs, a dull ache spreading behind his eyes. Was he as bad as his father? Because he did not want to let Syra go back to the tundra either.

"I should go to bed," he said, standing from the table. "I have a headache."

"I've always been proud of you, boy," Yefrem said as Viktor walked away. "I hope that one day you'll be proud of yourself."

Climbing the back staircase, Viktor wiped at his stinging eyes and silently cursed his growing headache. He told himself it was from exhaustion: he had been up since before dawn.

Emerging on the second floor, he hesitated before Syra's closed door. He thought of the way she held his shoulders – like he steadied her – when he kissed her. What he wouldn't do to feel her lips and hands on him again. But the shame and the guilt ate away at him until he was only a husk. A shadow unworthy of Syra's touch.

His chest tightened. Yefrem was right: he could do right by her and maybe then he might be worthy of her. And to do right by her, he could start with the truth. That Lord Igor Sviatopolkovich didn't just want momentary aid but a lifetime of service.

He knocked gently at the door.

The door creaked open a finger's width.

"Syra?" Viktor peered into the unlit bedroom and then pushed the door open just enough so he could slip in.

Dressed in one of his tunics, Syra slept on her back, her arms curled above her head like a dancer's. Viktor sucked his teeth, letting his gaze climb her bare legs. She was beautiful, and his palms burned with the desire to touch her.

But it was clear that she hadn't opened the door.

Her pack and reindeer hide clothes littered the rug beneath his feet. Still in its pocket in her bibs, the Bone Doll glowed. Then, it was as though he were a puppet who another controlled. He knelt down. He smelled iron – no, *blood* – and his arm extended of its own accord towards the Bone Doll. The thing *twitched*. And though he knew he shouldn't, he touched it.

The world went dark. And Viktor felt like he was falling from a great height, the wind roaring in his ears. Then, silence, stillness.

"She pities you," a voice that sounded like his own whispered from behind his shoulder.

Viktor spun, but there was nothing there. Just the dark and the empty. He turned back around and came face-to-face with *himself*. His double was wearing the same clothes, but they were cleaner and better fitting as though this version of himself had succeeded in life.

"You don't want a woman," his double said. "You want a prize. A pretty bauble to parade around. To prove you're not a pathetic wretch." His double stalked forward. "You are a villain. You ruin everything you touch. What do you think you will do to her?"

But then it wasn't his double that was standing over him. Syra stood there, her eyes lifeless. A heavy chain wrapped around her neck, leaving bruises in its wake. Viktor reached for her but his fingers slipped through her like she was a ghost.

"No!" he shouted and then, suddenly, the bedroom had returned. He was lying on the floor, shaking, while the Bone Doll sat across the room, glowing faintly blue.

Syra – the *real* Syra – knelt over him. Gently, she ran her hands along his face and throat, then across his chest, before examining his hands. Viktor held his breath to stop himself from doing or saying anything stupid, but damn it, he wanted her to touch him like that again – and *slower*. "Are you hurt?"

"I'm fine," he stammered, though his heart was beating so hard he thought he might die.

"I told you not to touch it." She cupped his face. "It could have burned you or worse."

Viktor would have taken a burn over what he had seen. But he didn't mind Syra touching his face. Reluctantly, he sat up. "I think I got the 'or worse' part."

She glanced across the room, where the infernal artifact flickered brighter for a moment as though recognizing her gaze. "Don't believe anything it tells you. It's not true."

But what the Bone Doll had told Viktor *was* true. *You ruin everything you touch.* He placed his hand on her collarbone, slipping his fingers beneath the cool beads encircling her throat. Her pulse fluttered beneath his thumb.

"It's late." Taking his hand, she stood and then guided him to his feet. "And we both need rest."

Viktor swallowed. He had come to tell Syra the truth, and now was the time. He squeezed her fingers, willing himself to be brave. It would only take a few simple words.

But then Syra unfastened his belt, letting it fall to the floor. Next, she easily undid the buttons on his caftan. Shrugging off his undertunic, he stood before Syra, who ran her hand appreciatively up his bare chest from navel to heart. Heat bloomed across his skin.

It was then he knew he couldn't tell her. He held his breath, afraid even the slightest movement might ruin this. He wanted her to touch him *forever*. And if he told her the truth, she would be upset. She would be angry at him for lying. She might even leave, returning home without his help. He couldn't risk any of that. He needed her hand on his naked chest, resting above his racing heart.

She kissed him on the cheek and then led him to the bed where they slept chastely side by side, half-dressed.

CHAPTER 14

The Screamer

Viktor was already buttoning his caftan when Syra opened her eyes. She stared at him a long moment, trying to reconcile the warmth in her bed and the almost fully-dressed man before her.

"Zoldrovya is three days south of here." He adjusted his sleeves, avoiding her gaze. "I'll help Yefrem pack the supplies."

She cocked her head to the side. No Sarnok man would sleep chastely beside his new woman, wake up, and simply *get dressed*. Was that a Ruthenian habit? Or was it only Viktor?

"Why did you touch it?" she asked, wishing he would stay.

Viktor went still, his hands frozen midway through buckling his belt. Then, as though making a conscious effort, he continued. "Your door was open. I thought perhaps you were awake. But you were asleep and the Bone Doll was ... moving."

Her hairs stood on end. "You should have left."

Viktor looked stricken as though he couldn't fathom the thought of leaving her in the room with the half-sentient Bone Doll. The pang in her chest sharpened. He cared about her in a way she had never expected.

"The Bone Doll called you." Syra climbed off the bed and padded towards him. It called her family, her clan members. It gave them nightmares. It lured the youngest children and the animals away from camp. Now, it was doing the same to Viktor. "It will try again. You have to resist it."

"It's three more days to Zoldrovya," he said. "I'll be careful."

"And on the return journey," Syra said. "You will be the one to take me back, right?"

"Of course," he said with one of his odd smiles. "But you will need to defeat the *leshy* first."

Syra knew that Viktor preferred the road, but she didn't like the idea of staying in Zoldrovya while he went off on more errands. "Will you stay with me, in Zoldrovya, while I bind the forest spirit?"

His smile faltered. "I will, at the beginning. But I … may be pulled away." He turned from her. "I should pack."

Syra wanted to reach out and hold him. But it was pointless. Whether they left now or this afternoon, they would still arrive at Zoldrovya in the end. Whether she had enough power to bind the *leshy* or not, she would return to the tundra. And Viktor would return to his solitary travels. Holding him here wouldn't change any of that.

Besides, he didn't seem to want to stay.

She stared at the door after he left.

Enough moping, she told herself. She dressed in the plain, gray clothes left for her, grateful they weren't as heavy as her now too-warm reindeer hides. She tucked the Bone Doll into the heavily scuffed belt purse before heading downstairs.

After breaking their fast with Yefrem, eating white bread and fresh eggs, she and Viktor left the old man and the stone house behind. They walked in silence through the city of Beluvod, which was alive and swarming like a hornets' nest just like the day before, then through miles of fields where men and women were burying seeds in the dirt. And finally, by late afternoon, the road returned them to the forest.

Though different from the tundra's wide expanses, the forest calmed Syra with its quiet. And it was beautiful with its shades of blue, gray, and green. After Beluvod's cacophony, returning to the solitude of nature felt like the sweet music of a reed flute.

"This road goes from Beluvod to the great city of Khirzan," Viktor said, "which is where the Grand Prince lives. More than 60,000 people live there, not including the serfs and peasants living outside the walls."

Beluvod was already impossibly large. A larger city was simply unfathomable. Syra shook her head in disbelief. "Have you been there?"

He shook his head. "I've been to Rodgorod in the north, but I have not gone very far south or west."

"*This* is very south," she said.

"Compared to the tundra, I suppose it is," he said with an easy smile. "I should go. I've heard that Khirzan has an emporia unlike any other, where Bolghar, Skanians, Greshkaya, Abbasids, Tang'ans, and even Makurians come to trade..."

Syra stopped listening as her belt purse twitched. The Bone Doll. It jerked harder this time, making her belt cut into her hips. And then it began whispering in a language all its own, its voice urgent. Fear settled in her stomach like a block of ice.

"Viktor–" she began, just as his stride faltered.

"Do you hear that?" he asked.

The air hung still.

Then, an unearthly scream shook the forest. Syra covered her ears as the sound pierced into her bones; and, a step ahead, Viktor staggered. By the time the scream stopped, Syra was nauseous, her ears ringing.

It came from behind.

A great force pulled Syra's pack, hauling her backwards. Her backside struck the dirt and she was dragged across the road, into the thicket, through the trees. She thrashed, trying to get away, but her pack's straps trapped her arms. Something tore in her shoulder, radiating pain down her arm and into her chest. Crying out in pain, she caught a glimpse of the creature attacking her – a hairless, bone-thin monster with long limbs. The thing screamed again; and Syra's vision blurred as her bones turned to liquid fire. Everything turning fuzzy, Syra felt for her knife. If she cut herself free...

A black form launched from the forest. Viktor. A knife gleaming in his hand.

He slashed the beast across its forearm in a spray of inky black blood. The creature dropped Syra and rounded on him. Its head was unnaturally large for its thin body, its face a wrinkled mass of skin. It screamed, the force of its voice visible as it knocked Viktor off his feet.

Her entire body throbbing, Syra cut herself free from her pack and then crawled a few inches away. She tried to recite her grandfather's chant, but she couldn't hear anything over the creature's scream. The Bone Doll jerked again. She ripped open her belt purse.

As her fingers closed around the doll, the world went dark.

And then exploded in blue light.

The source of the blue light was ... her. It was as though Syra hung in the sky, watching her body below. The Bone Doll clasped in her fist, she hovered above the ground as bright blue light spilled from her mouth and eyes. Syra – or her body – turned towards the screaming creature. Her body snarled incoherent words, the blue light frothing from her lips, and the beast recoiled. Her arm raised, holding the Bone Doll above her head.

And then the monster fled.

The light vanished like a candle's flame that had been blown out, and Syra's body crumpled. Then Syra was falling. All the way from the sky. She opened her eyes – *in her body* – and gasped.

Viktor knelt beside her, concern painted across his features as he cradled her head. "Are you all right?"

"I'm fine." Or at least Syra thought she was. Nothing hurt – not even her shoulder – and the Bone Doll lay on the ground just out of arm's reach. She sat up. "You saved me."

"That thing grabbed you," he said. "And I almost lost sight of you. And then I thought that thing was going to kill me. And then you were glowing." Viktor clasped her face between his hands. "Fuck, I was so worried."

Then, he kissed her.

His fingers tangled in her hair as he cupped the back of her head; and Syra let him drink his fill from her mouth. She ran her hands up his chest, relishing the feel of his lean muscle; and he groaned. Viktor's free hand slipped beneath her tunic, his thumb tracing shimmering circles against her skin.

"I want you," she whispered as he trailed kisses down her throat.

Syra witnessed something inside Viktor break. His brow furrowed as though she had both destroyed and rebuilt him in the same breath. He kissed her again, slowly this time and deep as though offering a piece of himself.

"You're beautiful," he said when he came up for air, tracing the shape of her lips.

"Are you trying to flatter me?" she said, her tone half-teasing and half-needy.

He groaned, bending his head to her neck. His mouth was warm, his teeth gently as he nibbled her delicate skin. And then he found her mouth again, kissing her so hard that she forgot where she ended and he began. She wrapped her arms around him and held him tight.

And they kissed and kissed and kissed – a tangle of mouths and hands and moans – until they both came up gasping for air.

The air smelled of fallen leaves and spring flowers; and the birds were twittering away around them. Syra couldn't remember the last time she had felt this good. But all good things came to an end. Kissing him one last time, she stood and then helped him to his feet.

CHAPTER 15
The Lord of Zoldrovya

Viktor's stomach hardened with every step he took down the narrow path that turned eastward. He was certainly the worst man alive, leading his unknowing lover to her doom. He had meant to tell her that his father meant to keep her, so that his father could control the *leshy*. But every time he tried, his throat constricted and he thought he might choke. Syra liked him. She *wanted* him. Her touches were like a dream from which he never wanted to wake. And he couldn't bring himself to tell the truth and ruin what little time they had.

Syra would hate him soon enough.

"What's the matter?" Syra touched his hand.

"Nothing." Viktor smoothed his features. "I was just worrying about that thing we saw on the road."

"You've never seen it before?" she asked.

He shook his head. "It was a screamer. I've never seen one. But I've never seen a *rusalka* either."

"The forest is angry." She narrowed her eyes at the birch trees with their golden-green leaves. "Maybe it senses the Bone Doll."

"It's not the Bone Doll," Viktor said. "The forest has been angry for a long time."

The effects of the forest's fury became apparent as they approached the manor house. The manor was half-ancient kremlin and half-new manse where generations of building clashed and melded together into an architectural monster. And while the manor used to have several acres of lawn and pastureland, now the forest closed inward. Trees and bramble stole the lawn and grew all the way to the house's foundation; and thick ivy clawed its way up the walls, swallowing half the building. All that growth had happened in the past three years; and no matter how much Lord Igor's serfs fought the forest, it grew back greater and closer.

Viktor explained it to Syra in hushed tones.

Her eyes widened and her lips parted as she scanned the manor and its destruction. "*This* is the creation of one spirit?"

"The *leshy*."

"I don't know if I can dispel this creature," she said.

"You've managed the *rusalka* and the screamer," he said.

She shook her head. "It's the Bone Doll. It has been pushing back those spirits, not me. Maybe the Bone Doll will fight the *leshy*, but I can't control it.

A hope flickered in Viktor's chest. If the Bone Doll forced the *leshy* away, then his father might send her back to the tundra for being unable to control the *leshy*. Then, Viktor's lies would come true and Syra might never know of his deceit.

He bit the inside of his cheek. His father might not have wanted the Bone Doll's dispelling magic, but he might certainly put it to use. And Syra would still be stuck.

As they approached the manor, a servant greeted them and ushered them inside wordlessly. Though the forest encroached on the manor's exterior, inside looked just as it always had. The floor and trim were done in the golden-hued birchwood that gave Zoldrovya, meaning "Golden Wood," its name; and gilded murals depicting forest creatures shone in the sunlight trickling in from the windows. Everytime Viktor returned, he admitted that his parents' home would be beautiful if not for the oppressive sense of dread that suffocated him when he entered.

Lord Igor Sviatopolkovich sat on a red-upholstered chair in front of a colossal birchwood desk in the manor's study, a ledger and pen in his hands. He did not look up. "I sent you to find magic, and you come back with a tundra woman."

Viktor felt Syra stiffen beside him, and he took a deep breath. He had been too much of a coward to defend her in Kholm, but he could be different here. If only he mustered the courage to face his father head-on. "Syra is a Sarnok shaman. She carries a magical artifact that I think will work."

She glanced at him sidelong with a flicker of appreciation.

Lord Igor ran his tongue across his teeth. "All right, *moy mudak*. What *is* this magical artifact she has?"

Syra pulled the Bone Doll from her borrowed belt purse. As though it knew it was on display, the figurine lay dormant, looking like nothing more than an ornament. "This is the Bone Doll. My grandfather used it to bind spirits."

"But you don't?" Igor raised a critical eyebrow.

"Syra has defeated a *rusalka* and a screamer," Viktor said.

The lord slowly looked up, appraising Syra. "You have?"

"And a red creature," Syra said.

Viktor hid his scowl. When had she done that?

"An *upiór*," murmured Igor. He turned to Viktor again. "And this ... doll ... is the root of her power?"

"It strengthens her," Viktor said, though he wasn't sure if he understood how Syra's or the Bone Doll's magic worked.

"You do not need to speak as though I am not here," Syra protested.

Of course, Lord Igor ignored her. He resumed his perusal of the ledger. "This had better work, Viktor. I don't need another one of your failures on my hands. If the woman can't control the *leshy*, you will wish you weren't born."

Viktor remained perfectly still. He had endured brutal beatings and crushing humiliation at his father's hands. What more could his father really do? He just hoped that Syra would be ... treated well? allowed to return to the tundra? He just hoped Syra never faced his father's wrath, he decided.

Lord Igor lifted a small metal bell that sat on the corner of his desk and rang it. "Leave. I have better things to do than speak to my worm of a son."

Viktor stared at the floor as a servant arrived, bowing obsequiously before guiding him and Syra from the room. He dared not look at her. He wasn't ready to see her shock, her disappointment. He clung to the sound of her voice as she told him *I want you.* He would much rather hear that than talk about how he had lied to her for three entire weeks. His dread slowed his heart and weighed down his limbs.

Syra stopped, pressing her hand to a vine-covered window. She didn't move, even when the servant turned back and raised his eyebrow at them.

"Give us some space," Viktor said tightly, and the servant walked a dozen feet away. Viktor turned to Syra. He couldn't meet her eyes. "Syra?"

"You said Lord Igor was your employer."

"He is. In a way." Viktor rubbed the back of his head. He hated that flat tone she had. He wished he had told her the truth sooner. "I do what he says, and he gives me a supply of silver."

"But that was a lie."

He winced. "I don't relish my familial relationships. I try to … forget."

"You wish you were someone else," she said. "You want it so badly that you pretend to be someone you're not."

Yes. He wished he was someone that Syra *wanted.* He wished he was someone *deserving* of her. Lord Igor's son was a coward and a weakling. Syra was so strong, so intelligent. She didn't deserve a failure.

"I have been myself." He put a hand over his heart and lied. "Everything I have done has been honest. I just don't want to talk about my family."

"*Yourself* isn't employed by a lord. *You're* a lord," she said. It was an accusation "Why didn't you tell me? What would that change?"

He finally met her gaze, his expression miserable and his shoulders sagging. "Truly, it started off as me just not wanting to talk about my family. But then I worried that you might not like a Ruthenian nobleman. You liked me … as I was. And I liked you. I didn't want anything to change."

"You have to tell people the truth," Syra said.

Viktor stepped forward, brushing her black hair away from

her face. "I will," he promised. *Somehow. Eventually.* "From now on, I won't keep anything from you."

She leaned her cheek against his hand. "Is there anything else you haven't told me?"

He knew he should tell her about his father's true intentions. But he loved the feel of her warm, brown skin against his palm and the way her eyes searched his face. He wanted to hold this moment forever. He would tell her everything later.

"No."

CHAPTER 16

Amongst Family

Pausing before the golden-hued doors, Viktor straightened his caftan. Almost losing Syra was second worse only to dining with his family. If he *had* lost Syra because of his stupid lies, that would have been worse. But she still – tentatively – liked him, wanted him. And right now she was safe in her guest room, so he could focus on how unpleasant it was to be home.

Clearing his throat, he gestured for the servants to open the door. The dining room was paneled and floored in birchwood, its ceiling painted a midnight blue with constellations dotted throughout. A long, cherrywood table stretched the entire length, though only five places were set – all clustered at the eastern end.

His mother Oksana Viktoryevna stood, sweeping across the room in her sapphire-blue *svita* to dramatically embrace him. She was tall and slender with her copper-colored hair dressed in a wimple. "Oh, Vitya! You look so tired!"

Viktor dutifully kissed both of her cheeks while his father remained seated, leaning casually back in the dining chair.

His sister Irina, a red-haired woman of twenty-five with a perpetual pout, patted her younger sister's arm and said, "Anna and I took bets on whether you would die out there, poking around for forbidden magics."

Viktor offered his blandest smile. *How pleasant.* He already wished he was back on the road with Syra. She was at least honest with her emotions.

"Come and sit." Oksana shoved him into a dining chair and then foisted a goblet of cinnamon-spiced wine on him. "You have been on the road so long. I'm sure you haven't had a proper meal in months."

"I am used to road fare," Viktor said politely.

Lord Igor interjected. "I think she's played you, *moy mudak*," Igor sneered. "I gave you the best education money could buy, and you still still cannot tell a woman from a dog."

Viktor's anger flared. "Syra is not–"

"My dear Gosha, you're upsetting me," complained Oksana as her two daughters watched the scene like cats who had cornered a mouse. "Let's talk about something more pleasant – like how Irochka will marry Lord Kyrill Petrovich's son this summer?"

Igor harrumphed, muttering something about their southwestern neighbor and his soldierly son.

His sisters, though, were clearly tired of hearing about the betrothal. Her red-gold hair plaited in two waist-length braids, Anna leaned forward. "Tell us about the tundra woman. Is she a noble lady?"

"Is she a whore like Pa says?" Irina said with an evil smirk.

"Does she speak Ruthenian?"

"I bet she's good with her tongue."

"Is she brave? Or timid?"

Viktor forced his jaw to unclench. He had always frozen or hidden from their taunts, but Syra deserved better than this. *She deserves better than me.* He forced that thought away. "Syra is a shaman, and the artifact she carries can control spirits."

Irina laughed shrilly. "You're fucking her!"

His face burned. He wished.

"Vitya," his mother whimpered, her eyes wide and shining. "You are ... *bedding* ... that woman?"

"I didn't say that," he protested. "Irina is jumping to–"

Oksana's face crumpled and she pulled out a kerchief. She began a peculiar sob – without tears. "Oh, my poor baby boy! Led astray!"

"You are a Ruthenian nobleman," growled Igor. "The son of a *boyar*. And you debase yourself by fucking that peasant."

Viktor wished his cheeks would stop getting hotter. He

hadn't crossed any line with Syra. He had treated her like a lady. "Don't talk about her like that."

"I should disown you," his father threatened. "All you've ever done is embarrass me."

"Do it." Viktor stood. "Disown me. That would be better than having to listen to you."

"*Get out!*" roared Igor.

Viktor didn't need to be told twice. He stalked from the room and slammed the door behind him. In the corridor, he paused. The servants stared at him in shock. He let out a sharp breath. He had never fought back before. It felt … good. If he could denounce his parents, he could surely tell Syra everything now.

He ran his fingers through his hair, nodded at the servants, and then went to find Syra.

CHAPTER 17
The Charade

Syra touched the wall in her room. Even inside, she could feel the *leshy*'s fury. Crushing, oppressive. It seemed like a strange companion to the vast emptiness inside her.

She wanted to be with Viktor. To kiss him. To do more than kiss him. But he had lied about who he was. She tried to understand why. His father seemed entirely unpleasant, and Ruthenians seemed to place quite a deal of import on nobility. But she could not quite understand how his parents would change how she saw him. Viktor was kind and generous and aspiring to be better. Not to mention striking with his orange hair.

She told herself that she forgave him, though she still felt a little hollow inside.

A knock sounded at the door and she turned. Viktor entered, smelling of wine and cinnamon. That hollowness shrunk, and in its stead, a soft warmth glowed. She stepped closer and placed a chaste kiss on his lips. He tasted just how he smelled, and it left her tongue tingling.

He caught her about the waist, sending trills of heat through her, and lowered his mouth to her ear. "Don't fight the *leshy*."

Syra stiffened. "What?"

"Please, don't fight the *leshy*." He drew her close like a lover, but his words were not sweet. "Leave."

"My Pathfinder is expecting silver." She pulled back an inch, trying to read his expression. "And your- your father said if I didn't bind the *leshy*, you would wish you'd never been born."

"Don't worry about me," he said, pressing his forehead to

hers. "I care about you."

She wriggled further back. Something was wrong. "What are you talking about?"

Viktor looked as though she had shoved her hand into his chest and squeezed his heart *hard*. "I want you to go home, so don't fight the *leshy*."

"I'll go home once I've faced it," she said.

He shook his head. "The Bone Doll will win. And you can't win."

"Viktor, I don't understand."

Anguish painted his features. "My father wants to control the *leshy*."

"The Bone Doll will push it back," she said. "It will be its own creature, but it won't be close enough to harm your house."

"My father wants to enslave the *leshy*," Viktor said.

Syra went utterly still, her thoughts tangling. "He wants to *trap* the *leshy*? He wants to bind it to an object? He wants to control it?"

"Yes," Viktor said.

"Why?"

"To make the forest bend to his will," he said. "What lord can say they control the trees and the vines and all the wild things in their lands? He wants power, like every Ruthenian *boyar*."

The Bone Doll twitched in her belt purse.

"He needs to bind it to something," she said. "Like the Bone Doll. But I can't make talismans. I'm not strong enough."

"That is why I want you to leave," Viktor said. "He would want you to stay to control it. And he would control you. Go back to the tundra before he has reason to stop you."

She staggered backwards, overcome with nausea. "You knew this. You led me more than 150 miles from my home, knowing I would never see my family or my clan again. And you didn't tell me."

Viktor averted his gaze, his arms hanging limply at his sides.

"What else haven't you told me?" Her fingers closed around

the beaded necklace. It was a chain, trapping her, leashing her. "What else have you lied about? Were those touches, those kisses all ploys? Keep me distracted so I didn't realize you were taking me prisoner?"

"I didn't lie about anything else," he said quietly. "I just wanted you."

Syra stared at him for a long moment. She knew Viktor admired the heroes in his stories and wanted to emulate them. But this... He had fashioned an entire charade so that she *liked* him, *wanted* him back. When he *knew* he was taking her prisoner. When he *knew* she should hate him. The necklace snapped, the beads falling to the floor.

Viktor knelt to pick them up.

"I can't trust you," she said.

"Syra, please," he whispered, refusing to meet her gaze.

"Leave." Her voice broke. "*Leave.* I'll deal with the *leshy* and your father myself. Go ... do whatever it is you actually do when you aren't lying. Because I never want to see you again."

CHAPTER 18

The Green Man

Syra slumped onto the bed, scrubbing at her wet cheeks. She was a fool. How did she not realize that Viktor was seducing her? The glass beads spread all over the floor. He had even said that necklace was a bribe, and she had forgotten about it just because she liked his kisses. She groaned and wished she could claw her own heart out. Maybe that would stop the pain.

While she was sniveling like a broken-hearted teenage girl, the door swung open. Lord Igor Sviatopolkovich strode in, a smug grin twisting his features, followed by a slew of guards. He stopped before the bed and crossed his arms in front of his barrel-like chest.

"It looks like my son had the balls to end it with you," he said. "A Ruthenian lord really is too good for a tundra bitch. But *I* still have need of you, and I won't even degrade myself by fucking you."

She fisted the covers, glaring at him.

"My son says you – or that little figurine of yours – has magic," Igor said. "And I need help with the *leshy* trying to tear down my house."

"I'll send him deep into the forest," Syra said.

"No, no, no." The lord wagged a finger. "You will bind him to another one of your figurines. And if you can't do that, you'll control it yourself. You and the *leshy* can be my little pets. It will be wonderful to control what grows where, and always have perfect hunts."

"You don't want the Bone Doll here," she said. "It's–"

"But I do," he insisted. He gestured to the guards. "And all these lovely men are here to make sure that you ensnare the *leshy*, just as I want, and return to me."

Three guards strode forward. Two grabbed her arms and hauled her off the bed, while the third pressed a knife into her lower back. Syra trembled but not from fear. Anger burned in her stomach.

"Take the girl into the forest," Igor ordered. "And make sure she returns."

They marched her out of the dining room and through the manor's maze-like corridors. The Bone Doll reverberated in her belt purse, as angry as she was. Shadows and creeping vines reached out to meet her; the guards hacked the latter away. A soft mist climbed up from the loam below their feet, obscuring the forest floor. And they kept walking her deeper and deeper in until she could no longer see the sky above.

Finally, the guards let her go with a hard shove. Syra almost lost her footing but caught herself. Stepping hurriedly away from them, she drew the Bone Doll, her knuckles turning white as she gripped it. It was painfully hot against her skin, but she didn't let go. It had saved her from that screamer; hopefully it would protect her here. She looked around slowly. The fog began to twist tightly around her, turning the forest almost black. The nearby owl went silent.

I don't want to do this...

Then, she heard choking. Thick vines wrapped around the guard's throats. Their faces turned redder and redder as they kicked out against the loam. But the vines did not unrelent. The guard on the left dropped, limp and purple-faced. A few moments later, the vines dropped the second corpse and the third. The other guards, further behind, backtracked hurriedly until she could neither see nor hear them.

In her fingers, the Bone Doll glowed blue.

A figure emerged from the forest.

Her eyes widened as it moved forward into the moonlight. It was a man who seemed nearly as tall and thick as an oak tree. He wore a long, green caftan over matching trousers. But he seemed to misunderstand buttons: the front of his caftan was twisted and pinched from his attempts to put buttons in the wrong holes. And when Syra stopped trying to understand his odd dressing habits, she noticed the shining and sharpened antlers that grew from above his ears.

"Who are you?" she demanded as the Bone Doll went dark, cold. "What are you?"

"I am the trees, I am the moss, I am the lianas that crisscross," the creature said in a voice as deep and dark as the underworld. "I am the lord of the golden wood, the soul of the birch forest."

"You are the *leshy*," she said.

"You are a woman far from home," he replied. "And you carry a creature from far away."

"The bones of a sky spirit," she said.

When the *leshy* shook his head, it sounded like a tree creaking in the wind. "It is a spirit of the sky, to bone long ago tied."

In her hand, the Bone Doll twitched and glowed brightly along its carvings as though agreeing to the forest spirit's assessment. Syra scowled. She had been carrying around a *living spirit* this entire time?

"It tries to force your hand," he said. "It attacks those that do not have the power to fight it."

The curse. The nightmares, the whispers, the dead reindeers and the almost-missing children. The Bone Doll was *threatening* them. And Lord Igor wanted to do to this *leshy* what her grandfather had done to the sky spirit. What would the *leshy* do if imprisoned by a human?

"The lord" – she gestured to the manor behind her – "wants to control you. He wants me to bind you to something, like the Bone Doll."

"You cannot do it," the *leshy* said.

"No." But maybe dispelling it was enough. "But my clan needs the silver. And you have ruined the house here."

The *leshy*'s eyes burned and crackled green. And then there was nothing there – just empty eye sockets, a vine crawling out of one and trailing down his cheek like a tear. "Be careful what you try, human. I am as ancient as the forest. I have been here since the first seed fell to the dirt, and I will be here until this forest is nothing but ash. I will not be forced."

She held the Bone Doll close. Spirits weren't meant to be leashed by humans. And this one – the one helping her – had been trapped for years. She stared back at the *leshy*'s increasingly tree-like face and opened her mouth to chant.

Then, a vine curled around her throat, lifting her off the ground. She choked, her eyes bulging. She tried to tell the *leshy* she *wasn't* going to ensnare it, but she couldn't speak. Black clouds burst in her vision.

"You are flesh, and you are bone," he intoned. "You will die. But I am the trees and the vines. I am the forest, and it is eternal."

As her vision flickered and darkened, she saw the night sky again – and the tundra below. Her brother and sister hauled something wrapped in reindeer hide out of their *mya* and set it on a sled that Syra did not recognize. They put bone beads and a fine bone comb atop the reindeer hide before bowing their heads and stepping back. An old man with webbing tattoos across his hands stepped forward, chanting and lighting a torch. A *sambana*. A death shaman. Syra began to cry. It was her mother in the reindeer hide. Dead.

Her consciousness blurred in and out, her throat bruising. She wanted to go home. She didn't want to be hundreds of miles south and west into Ruthenia's forests. She didn't want to be a fool, lured here by a pretty mouth and soft lips. She should have fought Munku's order. She wanted to be able to trust Viktor. Her fingers loosened. The Bone Doll fell. As the darkness gripped her, she heard it land softly amongst the dead leaves.

And then, a bright blue light exploded.

CHAPTER 19

Baba Les

Viktor stumbled outside. What had he done? Overhead, murky clouds threatened rain, and the trees stirred with a light breeze. He turned in a circle but found no direction to go. He couldn't stay here. Syra was here, and she never wanted to see him again. She had asked him, on the road, whether he wanted to see Khirzan. Maybe now was the time. At least it was a long walk *away* from her, so he could make her happy and at least do one useful thing with his life. And maybe he would grow so tired while walking that he eventually forgot about her.

Right now, he doubted it was possible. It felt like he would always want her.

Viktor punched the nearest tree. His knuckles split open. He truly ruin *everything* he touched. Just like the Bone Doll said.

Hissing through the pain, he shook out his hand. He wasn't thinking straight. He staggered through the trees and brush, trying to put some distance between himself and the manor. The forest pressed in around him. A pair of birds screeched at each other, but otherwise he was alone. He winced at the sight of his broken knuckles. Just another thing he ruined. He wiped his face on the back of his sleeve.

As he leaned against a tree, his breathing ragged, he heard a wooden creaking noise. Not trees, but like a makeshift door rattling in the wind. He frowned. He had thought the *leshy* had destroyed the servants' quarters years ago.

Against his better judgment, he walked towards the sound.

Amidst the trees, a ramshackle hut perched on stilts and

was surrounded by a fence made of branches. Chickens pecked in the yard, oblivious to Viktor's arrival; and a thin curl of smoke came from the chimney, smelling of pine and horseradish. Viktor hesitated. He didn't remember this place at all.

The door opened and an elderly woman stuck her head out as though she was expecting a visitor. She wore a patterned scarf on her head, wisps of iron gray hair poking from beneath it, and had two shining green eyes. She gestured to him. "Come, traveler, I have beet *shchi* on the fire."

Though his mind told him to be wary of strangers in the forest, his legs had other thoughts. Viktor stepped beyond the gate.

Her house was one room, with the fire on the northern side and a cot with a patchwork quilt on the southern side. And it was filled to the brim with all manner of things: vegetables like beets, cabbage, onion, sorrel; clay jars of every shape and size, some labeled and others not; a stack of blankets and a pile of rags; a spindle and a row of sewing needles strung on a thread; a collection of broken and unbroken stools; an array of spoons, ladles, and knives; the bones of squirrels and birds; and much more that Viktor couldn't catalog.

For the strangeness of her house, the old woman gave him a very ordinary bowl of *shchi* – beet soup flavored with horseradish and dill.

"I don't remember your house being here," Viktor said slowly.

She picked up a needle and began stitching two rags together. "Does the lord's son know every person on his father's land?"

Viktor licked his lips. "You're only two dozen feet from the manor house."

"You walked farther than you think," she said.

Viktor sat silently, then, unsure of what to say. The *shchi* was better than any of the food his family served; and it wasn't soured by his family's presence. His guilt only seemed to make him hungrier, and he finished it quicker than was polite. The woman didn't offer him more.

"You betrayed someone," she said, not looking up from her needlework.

Viktor flinched. "How do you know?"

"Your guilt is written in your eyes and draped like a cloak around your shoulders." She stabbed her needle into the ratty fabric with a certain cruel efficiency. "Did you lie to them out of love or cowardice?"

He swallowed. And though he wanted to get up and leave, his legs stayed rooted to the chair he sat in.

"You want to be like Dobrynya in the fairytales," she said. "But you are the *zmey*, stealing and burning whatever you see."

The *zmey*. A scaly, slithering, greedy thing. Perhaps a hero should come along and slay him.

Setting aside her needlework, the old woman slipped her withered hand into her apron pocket and pulled out a flat piece of glass. She settled in the palm of her hand and stared at it as though it were a mirror, though Viktor was certain all she could see was her palm.

"When you leave me, be careful which road you choose," she said. "In one direction is your fate. In another, your destiny."

Viktor scowled, standing. "Both paths lead to the same place?"

"The gods twist your fate from many fibers into a great rope," she said. "You can change what the threads are made of."

"Which way is which?"

She smiled and shook her head.

His skin prickled, and her magic finally released him. He jumped from his stool and backed towards the door. Then through it. He climbed down the front steps and trotted through the flock of chickens. The old woman didn't follow.

He glanced back.

The house on stilts, its yard, and the chickens were gone. Only trees and thorn bushes remained. The hairs on the back of Viktor's neck stiffened as he wondered if the woman and her house had been there at all. But the smell of horseradish and burning pinewood remained. Shaking himself, he turned away again, the forest shrinking closer. What did it matter if the woman was real or a trick of his desperate mind? Maybe if she was a spirit, she should have eaten him or taken him captive. Then, Syra would never see him again – and Viktor wouldn't have to walk away himself.

Just as he thought of her, a bright blue light flickered across the sky. He turned, his guts twisting. In the north, that bright blue light shone upward through the trees and into the sky.

"Syra," he whispered.

CHAPTER 20

A Bargain Made

Viktor ran until his legs gave out. And then he crawled, following the blue light through thorny underbrush and over twisted roots, until he found the bodies of his father's armsmen. Their necks were snapped, their faces purple and blue. Scrambling past them, he found Syra, her body hanging limply from a liana. Her eyes and mouth were open, pale blue light pouring from them like waterfalls. Dark spots floated in Viktor's vision. He reached forward and found not Syra but a caftan made from soft leaves and coarse bark.

The *leshy* turned. He was half-man, half-forest with fury carved into his wooden face. "She came to imprison me."

Viktor's muscles tightened, telling him to run. But he was too tired. And he would not leave Syra again. "It's my fault. I brought her here."

"She agreed."

Viktor swung his arm backwards towards where the armsmen were. "The guards forced her."

"They are dead."

The vine around her throat shifted. Viktor's vision blurred, his breathing rasped. If Syra died, he'd never forgive himself. "Please! Please, let her go. I lied to her. I didn't tell her that she was supposed to control you."

"She would chain me like she chains that sky spirit. But I will not be held."

"Let her go," Viktor begged. "Take me instead. I brought her here. I lied because I knew she wouldn't do it until she was forced. Spare her. And– And– Kill me instead."

A thick, woody liana wrapped around Viktor's throat. The *leshy* cocked his head, his neck creaking like trees in the wind. "Once, long ago, there was another who fought me for a woman's hand."

Viktor felt cold suddenly. "Lyoshenka."

"An arrogant and greedy man." The forest spirit smiled. His teeth were made from mushrooms and birch bark. "To marry the *kniazhna*, he promised the Grand Prince that he could bring back my head. He was weak and needed a peasant to help him. I let the peasant go. The knight is buried beneath my roots."

Lyoshenka from the stories had *failed*. He had wanted a woman better than him. And now he was buried beneath the forest. Maybe Viktor was *too* much like his heroes.

"I will never have Syra," Viktor said. "I don't deserve her: I'm a liar and a coward. I ruin everything I touch. Please, don't let me ruin her. Let me fix this one thing. Let her go home."

"I cannot promise her life," the *leshy* said. "That belongs to the sky spirit. Even now, it shields her from me."

Viktor watched the blue streaming from her eyes and mouth. The thing was *helping* her? Well, better to face the sky spirit later than have Syra die now. "Please, then let her go. You can have me. I am the heir to Zoldrovya. Kill me, and this all ends in a generation."

The lianas dragged Viktor forward until he was nose-to-nose with the *leshy*. "I would gladly end your desperate, little life. But your death will not rid the world of your family's scourge. You must. Take what is yours. Become the Lord of Zoldrovya. And bow to me."

Anything for Syra. "Okay, okay, yes."

The vines slackened, releasing Viktor. Then, slowly, they set Syra on the ground. Blue light still spilled from her, and she did not move. The *leshy* receded backwards, fading into the shadows. "Beware when you return home."

Viktor didn't pause to ask why.

He scrambled to Syra and wrapped her in his arms. Though purple and black bruises formed a ring around her neck, she was still breathing. His limbs weak from relief, he hugged her to his chest for a long moment, the sky spirit's blue light singeing his clothes.

Then, Syra began to spasm.

"Syra," he said. "Can you hear me? The *leshy*'s gone."

She began to speak, but not in a language he had ever heard. Pain etched itself into her features. Her spasms turned into shudders.

"Syra, please, come back." Viktor held her tighter, trying to stop the shaking. "I'm sorry. For everything. Please, just come back."

She – no, the sky spirit – started screaming. She thrashed, elbowing him in the gut and knocking him aside. Clambering onto her hands and feet, she scampered like a spider. Her skin turned pale, effervescent blue; and matching blue lightning streaked across the sky. He scrabbled forward, trying to grab her, hold onto her. He managed to grab a fistful of her tunic. And then the world went pitch black. Silent as the grave.

His double appeared, wearing a fine silver crown upon his head. Was this version of Viktor a *boyar* now? Or a Prince? The double was wearing the same caftan – slate gray overlain with dark blue vines – but it fit better and wasn't singed. The other-Viktor smiled thinly. "You're a pathetic coward. You could not even fight the *leshy*. You just begged like a dog."

"I'd rather beg on my knees than let her die," Viktor said. "Would you do that for her?"

"You want a pretty little bauble so bad?" his double sneered.

"She's not a bauble," he snapped. "She makes me better. She makes me want to *be* better."

His hand knocked against something cool and smooth. The Bone Doll. Inert and dark without its spirit. And then, the darkness faded, his double evaporating like a cloud. The forest returned.

Crouched amongst the bramble, the sky spirit – inside Syra's body – stared at him like a frightened deer. Climbing to his feet, Viktor stepped forward and held out the Bone Doll. "We'll let you go, I swear. But we need Syra to do it. So you have to let her go."

The sky spirit, through Syra, spoke again in its foreign tongue. And then, carefully, it lowered itself down to the forest floor and closed its eyes.

The blue leached from Syra, revealing her brown skin, and the lightning faded. Viktor hurried forward, scooping her into his arms. She was still breathing, still warm. Viktor buried his face in her shoulder, holding her like a drowning man to a raft. He knew she hated him. But he needed this moment. He needed to prove to himself that she was alive and safe.

Finally, he lifted his head. Her eyes were open and watching him. He swallowed. "I know you never wanted to see me again, but…"

Syra cupped his face.

"I saw the Bone Doll's light and–" His mouth was so dry. And pressed against her, his body ached for her. He pushed himself off of her and sat, but he couldn't make himself move far. "I'm sorry, Syra. I'm sorry I lied. I'm sorry I didn't tell you everything. And I'm sorry I wasn't strong enough to leave you and never come back." He hung his head. "But I couldn't let you die because of my lies."

"I thought I was never going to see my family again," she rasped.

"Let me take you home." He put his hand over hers, holding her fingers to his face. "Let me fulfill that promise at least."

Slowly, she sat. "I thought I was never going to see you again."

Then she wrapped her arms around his neck, pulling him tight. Sighing against her hair, he embraced her in return and let himself enjoy her touch for as long as she was willing to give it.

CHAPTER 21
What the Forest Wants

For a long time, Syra clung to Viktor and he to her. She didn't know what to feel. She hated him for lying, for taking her away from her family, for putting her in danger like this. She loved him for caring for her on the road, for offering to lay his own life down for her, for offering pleading apologies to her unconscious form.

Finally, she eased her grip. "Viktor, I–"

"I'm sorry, Syra," he said. "I'm sorry I lied. That I brought you all the way here. That I put you in danger."

"I know," she said, unsure if she could forgive him. "But I'm glad you came back."

"I'm glad I did too."

He brought her hand to his lips and kissed it. Her emotions tangled inside her. She wished she could be angry or relieved – not both and a hundred other emotions besides.

"The Bone Doll." It sat beside them, glowing faintly as though in reminder. "A sky spirit is trapped in there."

"I promised to free it," Viktor said. "But I don't know how."

"I don't either. But if I don't free it, it'll continue to curse whoever is nearby." Gnawing her lip, she picked the figurine up and turned it over in her hands. "And maybe it's right to do so. No one wants to be caged."

"What will you do?"

"I will think about it," she said, finally untangling from him. "There must be something my grandfather taught me. I just have to remember it."

"Will you let me take you home?" Viktor was covered in

leaves and small twigs, and Syra thought he was still handsome, though she did not quite trust him.

She nodded wordlessly and then, standing, offered him her hand.

He pressed her knuckles to his cheek, as though he knew that kissing them was too much right now. "First, if you'll let me, I promised the *leshy* that I would become the Lord of Zoldrovya."

She felt a sharp pang in her chest at the thought of Viktor becoming the lord, like his father. "Your father is a cruel man."

"They're all cruel," he murmured, letting her hand drop.

"You are not," she said. "Do not become like them."

He gave a sad smile. "I won't."

They walked solemnly back to the manor, which was covered from base to apex in thick ivy. New saplings had sprouted at its foundation; in time, they would bring the house down on itself. When they reached the door, they had to cut down vines in order to open it. Syra's pulse quickened. There would be no manor for Viktor to rule. Inside, the *leshy*'s fury grew more apparent. The vines had smashed in the windows and now climbed down the walls and across the floor. The manor had already been quiet, but now it was terrifyingly so. And dark.

They found Igor Sviatopolkovich in his study, his face a red and mottled mess.

"*What have you done?*" the lord bellowed, coming around the desk like an orca hunting seal. "You fucking idiot! I told you to control it, not–"

Syra drew her knife, but Viktor caught his father's wrist before the man could land a blow. "The *leshy* is the lord of the golden wood," Viktor said. "And it doesn't want you here."

"What do I fucking–?" Igor pulled back, but Viktor held on. "Let go, *moy mudak*, or I'll break your legs again."

Her lips curled in disgust. *Again?* She pressed her blade against Igor Sviatopolkovich's ribs. "Listen to your son."

"Tell your bitch not to bite," snarled the lord.

"Don't talk about her like that." Viktor shoved his father back, sending the man into the desk. "I was saying, the *leshy* doesn't want you here. If you don't want to be strung up on one of its vines, I suggest you leave."

"I am the Lord of Zoldrovya!" protested Igor.

"Not anymore," murmured Viktor.

Then, the vines on the floor began to writhe. Even Viktor scrambled back, putting an arm out to shield Syra. But the forest didn't want either of them. They curled around Igor, slithering and hissing almost like snakes. The lord roared for his son to help him, but Syra held Viktor's arm. The forest wanted Igor, and she would not win against the forest. And she didn't want to lose Viktor to it. Slowly, the vines dragged Igor across the floor and then through the window, the windowframe cracking as the lord's body broke through.

Syra squeezed Viktor's arm as he stared at the hole in the wall.

"I'm th-the Lord of Zoldrovya," he murmured. "I'm a *boyar*."

Her stomach sank.

"My mother," he said. "My sisters."

Syra stopped him. "What will you do?"

He glanced around as though looking for an answer. Finally, he said, "I'll send them away. Irina is engaged; and my mother and Anna can go to my uncle's estate."

Syra nodded, stepping back. As pale as winter snow, Viktor looked exhausted and broken. Part of her wanted to hold him and whisper sweet words into his orange hair. But her heart still ached from his lies. And no matter how much he might need her comfort now, she couldn't give it.

This would be a long night.

CHAPTER 22

An Honorable Man

With his mother and sisters sent away and the people who tended his lands settled, Viktor could finally bring Syra home. And though she should be happy, she just felt … numb. She wished she could kiss Viktor at night, but she hurt too much to even try. And in the end, he would need to return to Zoldrovya as its lord. Wasn't that for the best? She should not want a liar.

Viktor led them in reverse. Three days through the forest to Beluvod along the great, glass-like lake that was large enough to be a sea. They stopped at Viktor's townhome, where the old man Yefrem scowled and sighed over their story.

"The boy has many wounds to heal," Yefrem said when he caught her studying Viktor one evening.

Syra said nothing.

"Including wounds he inflicted on you, it seems," said the old man.

Part of her hated Viktor for dragging her through Ruthenia, his lies nearly killing her. But part of her still wanted him, those soft lips and his kind gestures. She slid her fingers over the Bone Doll. "He lied to me."

"Trust is hard to mend," Yefrem acknowledged. "But I think he will work his entire life to do it. The boy is fond of you."

Like a child was fond of their first reindeer? She folded her arms in front of her chest.

"When Viktor was a lad of maybe sixteen or seventeen, he caught the eye of a girl of about the same age," Yefrem said. "Her name was Yuliya, and he would have done anything for her. Lord

Igor noticed the pair, though, and decided to use Yuliya for his own purposes. Lord Igor always wanted Viktor to be more like him, so he paid Yuliya and her family to insist that Viktor prove himself a suitable match – or Yuliya would be forbidden from seeing him.

"They demanded that Viktor prove himself in a tournament. He could pick – hand-to-hand, wrestling, sword-fighting, archery. Viktor chose hand-to-hand. And while Lord Igor was certain that Viktor would be spurred on by teenage lust and finally find a propensity for violence, Viktor is not a violent man. His first opponent not only defeated him, but left him unconscious for two days.

"Lord Igor, of course, would not let that be embarrassing enough," continued Yefrem. "He paid Yuliya extra to come to Viktor in his sick bed and berate him for being a weak coward who could never defend a woman."

Syra closed her fist around the Bone Doll, which lay dormant in her pocket now, and wished she could fight people who were long gone. "That was a cruel trick."

Yefrem nodded before shuffling away.

Syra went to Viktor. He was carefully sharpening the gutting knife that she had gifted him. She touched her throat. She no longer had her beaded necklace.

"What sort of woman does a Ruthenian lord marry?" she asked. "The daughter of a Prince, like your knights?"

Viktor closed his eyes for a moment and then, not looking up, said, "There aren't enough Prince's daughters to go around."

She cocked her head. "The rest of you are unmarriageable?"

"We'll marry another noble," he said quietly.

"Your sister is engaged," Syra said. "Do you have an intended?"

When he looked up at her, Viktor was pallid with two rosy blooms on his cheeks. "I never proved myself worthy of a match."

"It's not about proving yourself," she said. "You are worthy just as you are."

Viktor shook his head and returned to sharpening the knife.

Once they had rested and Yefrem had secured them fresh supplies, Syra and Viktor continued northeastward. The next day, they stopped at Kholm; and Syra avoided the retaining wall where Viktor had first kissed her. For the most part, they didn't speak while traveling either, which reminded Syra of the early days of their journey. That made her sad, but she had nothing to say to Viktor and so remained quiet. After Kholm, she spotted the half-rotted hunter's hut where she and Viktor had lain back-to-back in the same bedroll.

And they kept walking.

She spent most of her days trying to remember any and everything her grandfather had taught her about making talismans like the Bone Doll. At night, she tried to read omens in the stars in case there was an answer there. After a few days, she thought she had pieces but not the whole.

In Vishnaya, the cherry trees had lost their pink blossoms and now wore bright green leaves. But the Bloom and Bramble Inn was exactly the same as she remembered: painted in bright red with a small tavern in the front. The same brown-eyed innkeeper greeted them, and offered them the same pair of cozy rooms.

But rather than retreating into her own room, Syra leaned against the doorframe of Viktor's room. She remembered aloud, "In the *banya*, there were two women talking about how pretty you are."

Viktor turned bright red, dropping his pack awkwardly on the cot in the far corner. "I am glad to serve as ... art ... for the people of Vishnaya."

"I thought they were right," she said.

He soothed the front of his caftan, his head lowered. His voice was quiet. "Back then I was sure you hated me."

"I hadn't wanted to leave my family," she admitted.

"And you were right to think so." He smiled brokenly. "I'm not much of an honorable man."

She considered him for a long moment. "You made a mistake. A grave one. But you are trying to right what you did wrong. Is that not honorable?"

"Syra..." Viktor met her gaze, his amber eyes gleaming. "I want to be honorable, I want to be brave, I want to be good. For you. But I don't want to be like Dobrynya. I don't want to give up my woman."

She pressed her hand to her chest, where her heart stuttered painfully. *His woman.* She held her breath as he stepped forward so she wouldn't inhale his cinnamon-scent.

"Do you hate me?" he asked.

She shook her head. "I just don't know if I can trust you. But perhaps I can try."

"I will do anything to earn your trust," he rasped. "I will beg. I will grovel on my belly. I will–"

Syra silenced Viktor with a finger to his lips. His cheeks turned a fetching color of red again; and his chest rose and fell along with his rapid breaths. "Always tell me the truth. Even when it's hard. And be Viktor. No one else."

He nodded.

Letting her finger drag down his chin and then throat, she leaned forward and then kissed him. She was soft and tentative at first, tasting the man who had both endangered and saved her. When he moaned against her mouth, desire flickered to light – hot and red inside her. Slowly, Syra folded her arms around his shoulders, deepening the kiss. He settled his hands on her waist.

Eventually, she sighed and pulled back, letting her gaze drift across Viktor's face. His bright eyes, his arched nose, his full lips.

"I want you," he whispered. "I love you."

"Love?" Syra echoed before kissing him again, her desire a deep thrum in her belly.

Viktor cradled her, kissing her back. His body was hard; and she pressed against him, relishing the feel of his wiry muscles. He felt like a man. *Her* man. She tangled her fingers in his orange hair, holding him in place as she savored his mouth. When their tongues brushed against each other, a gaping need opened inside her and she moaned. His grip tightened as though Viktor knew that Syra needed to *feel* him. He pressed her against the doorframe, then, and kissed her so hard and deep that she lost her sense of time.

Finally, they both came up for air.

Viktor rested his forehead against hers. "I am yours, Syra. Always."

They stood there, holding each other, for a long time, saying nothing.

CHAPTER 23

Her Bones Sing

Syra lay on her back in a clearing – with Viktor just across the fire – and traced the constellations in the sky. Like that night so many weeks ago, the stars aligned again. She knew now what it meant. A path, a journey. The Bone Doll hummed in her pocket almost contentedly, and she wondered if the Bone Doll had orchestrated this entire venture so that it could finally be free.

"My grandfather told me that he found the sky spirit's bones when he walked amongst the stars," she said. "And I remember him singing the chant he used to bind the spirit, to trap it in this doll."

Viktor propped himself up on an elbow, listening.

"That chant was to tether or marry," she said. "But there is a chant that releases or annuls."

"But you can't walk the skies," Viktor said.

"No," she said. "But maybe I can make a path. I just need a few things."

"In the morning?" he said.

"When we're a little closer to the tundra."

She turned over. Alongside the crackling fire, she fell asleep easily. And in the morning, they continued their journey. Beyond Vishnaya, the quagmire had dried; and if Viktor hadn't pointed it out, Syra would not have realized where they were. She was also much less angry at him this time through. Her distrust had melted into contentment; and Viktor strode through the wilderness like a wolf leading its pack. And if she did not need to find a way to release the spirit inside the Bone Doll, Syra might have asked to pause for a few days – or even a week – to relish their time together. Alas, though the Bone Doll remained quiet, she knew it would only be patient for so long before it no longer believed she would free it. So they maintained a quick pace through the forest. They overnighted again with Aron and his family in Bereza, sharing tales of their travels over horsebread and boiled turnips. And then they walked through the remainder of the Ruthenian forest to the edge of the tundra.

The sparse, yellow grass and patchy lichens spread as far as Syra could see, the gray sky endless above her. Only then did she hesitate.

Another week and she would be back in her family's *mya*. Another week and she would be sleeping between her siblings. Another week and she would be convening with the other *vidutanas*. Would it feel the same, though? Her mother was dead, killed by a long winter and a persistent cough. That would always be a hole in her life, like the empty spot where her grandfather used to be. Then, the Bone Doll would be gone – but that surely was a good thing. She wanted to go home. She had wanted it from the moment she had left. So why did the tundra seem colored by loneliness and trepidation?

Viktor stopped, turning back to look at her. "Are you all right?"

"I need to rest." She gestured to a trio of wide, flat rocks that protruded from the ground and then made her way towards it.

As she set her pack down on one of the rocks, Viktor rummaged through his. "Have some water and cheese. You'll feel better with food in you."

"Viktor." Syra shook her head, her fingers fumbling with the pin on her cloak. "I don't need food."

Viktor stilled like a rabbit spotted by a fox. A deep and almost painful-looking desire kindled behind his gaze. But he did not move, did not say a word.

"Come here," she whispered.

She stepped up to him, running her thumb along his jaw. His breath caught as she kissed him, his hands trembling as they found her waist. Moving back a hairsbreadth, Syra held his eye and then let each layer of her borrowed clothes fall away. Viktor's cheeks turned rosy as she turned her attention to him, undressing him slowly and laying kisses on his newly bared skin. Bending forward, he kissed her ear and then pressed his mouth to her throat – slowly, purposefully – making her sigh. Then, she tilted his face to her and kissed his mouth, deeper this time.

They found themselves on the cool, dry grass. Syra climbed onto his lap, her hands on his shoulders and his cock hard between them. She and he stared at each other, their breaths rasping in time.

"Okay?" she said.

He nodded, the need and vulnerability in his expression conveying more than words could.

Syra ran her palms along his chest, across the corded muscles in his arms. And Viktor touched her reverently, his fingers grazing the back of her thigh, the curve of her waist, the swell of her breast. Their kisses turned exploratory and worshipful: he kissed along the freckles on her collarbone; and she suckled the small scar on his bottom lip.

He groaned, his hips lifting, as her fingers wrapped around his cock and then guided him inside her. She shifted her hips unhurriedly, letting him sink deeper; and he exhaled as though she had knocked the wind out of him. He cupped her face with both hands, anchoring himself to this moment and to her. It made Syra gasp. She couldn't remember the last time someone had touched her with ... wonder. Letting herself groan in pleasure, she rocked against him slowly, her core melting with the heat of their coupling.

Viktor ran his thumb across her lower lip, and Syra kissed it.

"You feel like–" Viktor began and then moaned as she lowered herself down, pressing their bodies together.

Tingling pleasure trilled along Syra's skin as he kissed her collarbone, her throat, her mouth again – as though he was trying to memorize the shape of her through kisses. She arched into him, her nails digging into his chest. Not enough to hurt. Just to claim him. And his hips lifted to meet hers, making her whimper with every thrust from below.

Then, she felt it. It had been waiting for days. Maybe weeks. Maybe from the moment she saw his amber eyes and orangebush lichen-colored hair. Her bones began to sing, and her heart rushed like a winter gale. A tight spiral of need whirled within her, faster and angrier.

She gripped his shoulders harder, pressing her cheek to his as her breath broke. "Don't stop."

He shook his head, panting and fucking her reverently. Desperately.

When Syra came, it felt like being lifted up to the stars – and pulled to the depths of the underworld. Both. Crying out, she tightened her thighs around Viktor's hips and moved up and down him slowly, tearing herself apart while he watched with something close to awe.

Then, Viktor joined her, stiffening as he spent himself.

His arms wrapped around her – one hand tangled in her hair, the other splayed against her spine. "I love you," he murmured into her hair.

Syra pressed a kiss to his ear and admitted, "I love you too."

CHAPTER 24

Home

Y*ou feel like home,* Viktor wanted to tell Syra. That Zoldrovya, that Beluvod, that the road – none of it felt like her. And that a reindeer hide tent on the tundra was surely better than a manor in the birchwood forest – or a townhome in Beluvod – because *she* was there.

But Syra spoke nothing of a future. And Viktor was grateful enough for these past few weeks that he could not bring himself to ask for more. Besides, she surely had a full life to return to – and didn't need to add a Ruthenian man to the mix. So, he relished their evenings and mornings, which were full of storytelling and lovemaking; and during the daytime, Viktor bartered for supplies to bring back to the Lame Wolves – since the promised silver was not coming.

The clan had moved in the two intervening months, following their reindeer herd, which gave Viktor two more days with Syra. And in that time, Syra collected what she needed to release the sky spirit from the Bone Doll.

From deadwood, shed antlers, and grass twisted into twine, she fashioned a small sled. In its basket, she collected one of the tunics he had given her, her belt knife, and wolves' teeth that she cut off her reindeer hide coat. When she was ready, she lay the Bone Doll atop all the offerings. For the first time in weeks, its carvings glowed softly.

"Hold my hands," Syra said.

If Viktor understood correctly, the ritual was strongest with three people and weakest with one. While four was a sacred number in Ruthenia, three represented the sky, earth, and underworld for the Sarnoks – a world in balance. Hopefully, two – and one of them a Ruthenian – would work for this ritual.

Syra began the incantation.

The Bone Doll's light grew brighter and bluer, growing to encompass the entire sled. Then, the Bone Doll itself cracked, glowing red fissures opening across its surface until it opened like an egg. A strange creature – like a mix between a deer, an eagle, and a human – lifted from the remnants. Its hindlimbs landed on the sled's footboards, its forelimbs on the handrails. With a whispering sigh, the sled lifted off the ground. It hovered a few inches above the ground for a long moment. And then, the sky creature leapt upward, streaking blue and red until it vanished. The sled crunched as it struck the ground, the wood splitting and the ritual items falling to the dirt.

The sky spirit was free.

Syra kissed him then, and his head spun as he grasped her waist. He would stay here forever, if he had not promised the *leshy* that he would be the Lord of Zoldrovya. And if Syra would have them. She gave him several sweet, quick pecks and then took his hand, leading him away.

They left the sled and offerings to nature, and eventually, a cluster of *mya* and a cluster of reindeer appeared on the horizon, alongside a copse of spruce trees.

A reindeer herder spotted them first, but it was Syra's family – Viktor guessed by their keen resemblance – that greeted them first. Her sister threw her arms around Syra, kissing her repeatedly on both cheeks, while her sister-in-law and nephew waited their turn. Her brother berated her with a hundred questions. Syra flushed and grinned widely, answering about her adventures and the whereabouts of the Bone Doll.

And then their mood turned solemn as they spoke of Syra's mother, who had passed away. Viktor pressed his hand into Syra's lower back, holding her as best he could.

That was when Syra wiped her eyes and took his arm. "This is Viktor. He took me so far south that all there are are trees. He saved me from the *leshy*, and then he brought me back home."

Her brother narrowed his eyes at Viktor.

"I brought supplies." Viktor met the man's gaze easily. He would be gone in a few days, and her brother would never have to worry about him again. "My father promised silver in exchange for Syra's help, but my father is dead. I plan to make good on the promise, but in the meantime, I hope this can–"

The Lame Wolves' Pathfinder emerged from her tent – and the entire conversation started over again. Syra explained her part, and Viktor negotiated additional time to procure silver for the Lame Wolves.

When all that was done, he and Syra walked through the camp.

"You will stay in my family's *mya* tonight." She took his gloved hand in hers. "We will have fish soup."

"I saved rowanberries specifically for your family," he replied. "I hope they like them."

"It will be a feast."

"If you will have me," he said, "I can stay a few days. But then I have to return to Zoldrovya. For the *leshy* and … I'm sure I can scrounge up enough silver to pay what you're owed."

"No one defeated the *leshy*," she said softly.

"Still."

She slowed. "And once you get all this silver, will you come back here?"

"If you would like me to."

"I would," she murmured and then kissed him on the cheek.

Viktor wasn't certain what he felt – sadness, joy, or something else entirely. He didn't want to leave her, but he owed a debt to the *leshy*. And Syra had her own family and life here. Without him. But he would come back that one last time, for her.

Syra jerked her chin upwards. Though the sky was still blue, the moon had appeared and alongside it, a red star.

"That is goddess Zorya Vechernaya," Viktor said of the red star. "She opens the sky gates so that the sun can pass through them at night. When you see her in the morning, she is Zorya Utrennaya, the Red Dawn Maiden, who lets the sun into the sky and leads warriors to victory."

"No." Syra smiled. "That is the Lover. He is a man who fell in love with the moon. He climbed up into the sky to be with the moon, but the sky spirits blocked his path, refusing to let him cross to his beloved. They are forever parted, except on days when they both rise while the sun is still in the sky. We believe it's then that the sun protects them from the sky spirits' wrath and lets the two lovers meet."

"Syra, I…" His heart constricted. *I don't want to be like that.* "That's grim."

"I see the Lover as patient and steadfast." She squeezed his hand. "I will be like the Lover, waiting for the moon night after night."

Viktor swallowed. She thought an eternity of wanting, of yearning was admirable? For him, it was certain agony. An agony, he knew he must endure.

"But when you return again," Syra said, "I want you to consider staying here. Staying with me."

His eyes stung, and he blinked hard. "The *leshy*–"

"Does not need you all the time," she said. "Stay with me here when you can and … maybe I will go with you to Zoldrovya some seasons."

"Is that what you want?" he choked.

She turned to him, her eyes shining with tears. "Yes."

THE END

WANT TO KNOW WHAT HAPPENS NEXT FOR SYRA AND VIKTOR?

Find out in

The Wooden Heart

available on Amazon

or

for newsletter subscribers
(https://rebeccaganesh.com).

ABOUT THE AUTHOR

Rebecca Ganesh

Rebecca Ganesh is the author for the new romantasy series the Ruthenian Chronicle.

A professionally trained librarian, Rebecca spends their time gathering all the most compelling and erudite information to make their characters and world building pop.

Rebecca enjoys a good fantasy novel and is always on the lookout for new story ideas.

Connect with Rebecca:

Website + Newsletter: https://www.rebeccaganesh.com

Instagram: @rebeccathelibrarian

TikTok: @rganeshauthor

BOOKS IN THIS SERIES

The Ruthenian Chronicle

The Bone Doll

The Wooden Heart

The Malachite Maze (Forthcoming)

AUTHOR'S NOTE

Syra and Viktor's world is inspired by the histories and cultures of the Eastern Slavs and the Nenets, particularly during the Early Medieval Period. Scholarship in English is scant for both these groups, in particular the Nenets. I have tried my best to be respectful while also creating fictional people and cultures for a fantasy novella. I hope that the reader will give me grace where I took artistic liberties – either due to lack of information or for the sake of the plot or characters.

Please do not consider this novella authoritative on either of these peoples or their cultures.

www.ingramcontent.com/pod-product-compliance
Lightning Source LLC
Chambersburg PA
CBHW072033170626
46811CB00008B/3058